Welcome back to the romantic and magical place called Cozzi Cove, seven guest bungalows on the New Jersey Shore.

This summer, Cal and his new husband, Michael, along with sister, Taylor, and her wife, Carla, prepare for the first in the next generation of Cozzis. To add to the action: Cal finds his great-grandfather's diary, exposing a shocking surprise; Michael and Taylor weigh new job opportunities that could take them far away from Cozzi Cove; red-letter Christian and new houseboy, Billy Dean, gets his wish when meeting Jesus and John at the cove; summer guest, Nijad, can't decide which sibling he prefers—Annabel or Andrew; and Jonathan, an occult enthusiast, encounters a sexy vampire.

As usual, nothing is as it seems when romance blossoms once again at Cozzi Cove. What secrets, mysteries, and passions lie waiting to unfold? Find out in Book Four of the Cozzi Cove series.

Copyright 2017 by Joe Consentino

Published by
NineStar Press
PO Box 91792
Albuquerque, New Mexico, 87199
www.ninestarpress.com

Warning: This book contains sexually explicit content, which is only suitable for mature readers.

Print ISBN # 978-1-945952-78-4
Cover by Natasha Snow
Edited by Elizabetta

Praise for COZZI COVE

COZZI COVE: MOVING FORWARD:

"*Cozzi Cove: Moving Forward* delivers a strong cast of characters and a few surprising denouements to individual story lines that will bring a smile to your face and perhaps even a heartfelt sigh." *GGR Reviews*

"Who knew that 7 bungalows set surrounding a beautiful cove, could hold so many secrets, love and intrigue?" "The humour, whether subtle or not-so-subtle was superb, the timing delivered with perfection, Joe Cosentino is a natural comedian and another reason why I love reading his books. He is also very clever, he weaved moral messages throughout the entire storyline," "Great fun entwined with the Cosentino romantic magic that brings his books alive, I loved it." *Three Books Over the Rainbow*

"Visiting Cozzi Cove is like coming home or revisiting a beloved holiday destination. I know everyone, by now, who is a permanent fixture and I sincerely hope that Cosentino continues this series forever. As before, the characters are a hoot. They're a mixture of funny, quirky, sad, lonely individuals who come together to make a riotously brilliant cast." *Divine Magazine*

"Oh, Cozzi Cove, you are fast becoming a favorite vacation destination with your action and excitement! Joe Cosentino once again wins his way into your heart and soul with this fun, flirtatious romance. Love, laughter and smoldering intimacy await all who dare to venture to the clear blue waters of the Cove." *3 Chicks After Dark*

"I absolutely love this series and loved all of the romance that happens at Cozzi Cove. You don't just have one romance you have seven (really eight when you count Cal & Michael)." "I love an author that can inject humor in just the right places. Joe Cosentino is fast becoming a must read author for me." "I can't wait to read more from Cozzi Cove." *Inked Rainbow Reads*

"Imagine a beautiful getaway where the hot, sexy, and wealthy gay men go...it's a place where there's never a dull moment. Every page of this new title brings readers nothing but excitement, intrigue, and an intensity that will burn away the night's quiet. Most novels offer readers one journey in which readers travel upon, however, readers are brought not one but several journeys that will leave them breathless and hooked. As with all of Joe Cosentino's novels, humor comes in abundance and fits in perfectly with all of this stunning characters." "Joe sweeps his readers into his characters' lives by creating realistic characters with real issues. It's easy to get lost in it all. The book automatically captures your heart from page one and forever holds it. After reading the story, readers will be begging for the next grand adventure. Funny, heart melting, and swoon worthy, readers will finish reading this in one sitting. I loved reading this riveting tale, and I highly recommend it to readers everywhere." *Urban Book Reviews*

COZZI COVE: BOUNCING BACK:

"I loved this story. It carries you through the full range of emotions, from joy to sadness, from happiness to anger. The characters are beautifully written." "I look forward to a return visit to the Cove." *TBR Pile Book of the Month*

"Heartbreaking and heartwarming, sweet beginnings for some, sour endings for others, emotions jumping off the page as you turn eagerly to read more, welcome to Cozzi Cove. The author measured his scales to perfection in delivering the perfect balance of love, laughter and tears in this sexy, fun filled holiday romance entwined with some sadness. Summer magic waved its wand at all who visited and stayed at Cozzi Cove and I was one of those who wanted to stay." *Three Books Over the Rainbow*

"As a whole the story shines...the story is never dull and ends satisfyingly." *Elisa Rainbow Award Honorable Mention*

"I loved each character just as much as the next, each one had their own quirks and nuances. This was a great start to the series, and Jersey Shore has never looked hotter!!" *Alpha Book Club*

"In true Joe Cosentino style, this book is packed full of drama! This cast of characters will have you laughing out loud one minute before ripping your heart out the next." *Joyfully Jay*

"If you like a lot of angst, some humor, love, sadness (be sure to have a couple of boxes of tissue handy), and some hot sensual man-sex, I highly, highly recommend this book. I loved all of the Joe Cosentino's books, but I think this is my favorite to date! I am ready for book 2!" *Cathy Brockman Romance & MM Good Book Reviews*

"Joe Cosentino has the amazing ability to combine heartwarming, feel good moments with droll, sometimes biting humor, along with insights into the frailties and peccadillos of being human." "Cozzi Cove: Bouncing Back is the very finest in literary fiction with a romance theme, yet it's more than just that—it's about human connections and empathy and finding a way out of the fear and inertia faced by so many. It's also about courage and strength, about respect and coming to terms with all that life has to offer, and it's about letting go. I loved this book and look forward to the next in the series. This is a highly recommended read, well-deserving of Five Stars." *GGR Reviews*

"Readers will meet a variety of characters that creates a soap opera intrigue, unlike any other novel read. This story will definitely keep readers guessing with every page. Only when readers reach the last page does everything become known. It's addictive. Cozzi Cove is a brand new series that will keep Joe Cosentino's readers on their toes and begging for more. I laughed, cried, and fell in love with this latest novel." *Urban Book Reviews*

Cozzi Cove:

New Beginnings

Book 4

Joe Cosentino

DEDICATION

To Fred for everything over all these years; to Rae, Elizabetta, and the staff at NineStar Press, to my sister for those wonderful childhood memories on the New Jersey shore, to Jersey Shore lovers, and to the fantastic readers who begged for another Cozzi Cove novel.

AUTHOR'S NOTES

Cozzi Cove and the town of Cozzi are delightful figments of the author's imagination.

CHAPTER ONE

The sun rose like an erupting volcano filling the sky with shafts of violet, magenta, and gold, which ultimately turned to clear blue. Cal Cozzi stood on the white sand and gazed at the old lighthouse in the distance. At thirty-three, he was in the prime of his life, with thick auburn hair, clear green eyes, and a trim athletic build. Life was good, and as he smiled at the foamy waves teasing the craggy shore, Cal basked in the morning sun and in the beauty of his home.

Cal's great-grandfather, Calvin Cozzi I, had built the resort at Cozzi Cove and had had a big hand in the development of the town of Cozzi. It had always been home for Cal, and proved to be a solid oasis when as a young man his football and later restaurant careers failed, and nine years ago when his parents died in a car accident. He'd especially felt its comfort when he later lost his husband of five years to cancer. Like the bay water rejuvenated by the golden rays of each sunrise, Cal had put his life back together by managing Cozzi Cove and marrying Michael Rodgers.

It had only been a year since the greatest day of Cal's life, the triple wedding on the cove sands, attended by family and friends. Cal and Michael had been joined by two other couples in exchanging their vows: Cal's brother George and his longtime boyfriend, Aaron; and Cal's sister Taylor and her longtime friend, Carla. Though the Cozzi family was growing in numbers, Cal and Michael had wanted to start their own family right away. They did the happy dance on the sand when Carla offered to act as surrogate for their baby. With Carla's due date fast approaching, excitement, like the scent of the sea, filled the air at Cozzi Cove.

Michael, clad in a T-shirt and shorts like Cal, appeared at the front doorway of the main bungalow. His stocky build, caramel-colored skin, exotic eyes, and warm smile still caused Cal's heart to beat faster.

"I'm hungry."

"Then you'd better make breakfast." Cal enjoyed playing with Michael.

Michael liked it too. "If you make blueberry buckwheat pancakes, I'll give you a massage."

"You massaged something pretty well last night."

They shared a knowing smile.

Michael said, "I know how to get you inside."

"How?"

"The guests will be arriving soon."

At these words, Cal hurried inside the glass-enclosed porch, scooped the twenty-two-year-old into his arms, squeezed Michael's bubble butt, and gave him a good morning kiss. Then Cal went through the living room, passing the doorway to their front bedroom, and into the kitchen, glancing through the entrances to the rear bedroom and bathroom on the way. Cal was glad his brother's renovations of the bungalows had kept his great-grandfather's layout while expanding the rooms, including cathedral ceilings lined with white pine beams. As he gazed at the white wicker and oak furniture laden with flower-print cushions, Cal was thankful his great-grandfather's heavy nautical-themed furniture had found a home in a local museum. He smiled proudly at his own additions: the prints on the walls depicting lighthouses, seashells, and rocky beaches.

As usual, Michael leaned on the granite-topped island while Cal made breakfast. "Aren't you going to put more blueberries in the batter?"

Cal raised the mixing spoon. "Do you want to make these yourself?"

"I prefer to critique."

Cal mixed the buckwheat flour, buttermilk, egg, honey, coconut oil, and blueberries in a large bowl. "Your college degree is in photojournalism, not the culinary arts."

"A lot of good it did me."

"Your degree?"

Michael nodded and his soft chestnut bedhead fell into place. "Four years of college to be a bartender."

"You're only a bartender while Tommy is in New York City."

"Yeah, and when Tommy comes back from visiting Blue, it's bartender's assistant time again for me."

Cal poured the batter in circular mounds on the warm oiled skillet. "What about that gay magazine?"

"It was one freelance job!"

"Something else will turn up."

"Tell that to my resume on the web. It's beginning to feel like a wallflower at a party."

"It takes time. Photojournalism is a specialty field."

Michael pouted. That turned Cal on every time. He wrapped his arms around Michael and squeezed him into his chest. After a few wet kisses, Cal said, "You can always help me around Cozzi Cove."

"I thought you hired a new houseboy when Connor and his husband opened their bed and breakfast in town."

"I'm interviewing him this morning." Cal smelled the pancakes starting to burn. He grabbed the spatula and quickly flipped them.

Michael licked his lips. "You flipped me over like that last night."

"And you loved it."

They kissed again.

Cal felt Michael's erection pressing against his own. "I'd better concentrate on these pancakes." He slapped Michael's backside. "Instead of *these* cakes."

"That's not what you said last night."

Cal giggled and served the pancakes. They sat at the white oak kitchen table, feeding each other and intermittently licking maple syrup off each other's chins.

Just as they were finishing breakfast, Carla Mangione lumbered through the back kitchen door and announced, "If this watermelon doesn't come out of the patch soon, I'm going to kill someone."

"Hey, you're talking about *our* watermelon!" Cal replied as he got up to help her to the table. He put pancakes on a plate as Michael went to pour juice and milk for her.

"It won't be soon enough for me." Carla rubbed her enormous stomach; she was only thirty-five, but these days looked more like fifty-five. "I never knew you could get varicose veins on your stomach."

"And I'm sure yours are beautiful." Cal served Carla breakfast, kissed the top of her dark hair, and took a seat across from her at the table.

Carla leaned forward to massage her lower back. "I must be the biggest pregnant woman ever."

"That's because you're carrying our big, beautiful baby," Michael said, joining them.

After taking a sip of juice, Carla gagged. "Why does everything taste like fish or liverwurst?"

"Maybe our baby is the antichrist," Cal offered.

Carla took a bite of the pancakes. "What kind of huge genes do you two guys have?"

"Don't blame us." Cal put his arm around Michael. "It must have been the egg-donor."

"She must have donated ostrich eggs." Carla pushed her plate away.

Michael pushed it back in front of her. "Eat up, honey. You're having breakfast for two."

She looked down at her enormous stomach. "Really? Do you think?"

Cal finished his juice. "Whatever happened to, 'As your dear old friend and sister-in-law, it would be my honor to help you and Michael bring a child into this world. I can't think of anyone who'd make better parents'?"

"That was before I gained forty pounds and my back started aching constantly—before my breasts swelled up like helium balloons and my ankles expanded faster than a conservative politician's pocket after meeting with a Super PAC."

Cal fed her another piece of pancake. "But isn't it all worth it to bring a new life into the world?"

Carla groaned. "I used to get offended when people said God was a man. Now I'm sure of it. No woman would put another woman through this."

"Did you do your exercises this morning?" Michael asked.

Carla laughed. "I stopped being able to see my toes weeks ago."

"Have you been meditating with your crystals?" Michael sounded like a teacher with a lazy student.

"I think I threw them at your pictures when the baby kicked me like a Radio City Rockette. Meanwhile, you two were no doubt going at it last night like a running back and a wide receiver."

"A tight end, please," Michael said as he handed Carla her glass of milk.

"If I get any more milk in me, my breasts will explode." She took a sip and swallowed as if drinking fish oil laced with liquid soap.

Cal asked, "Have you been taking your prenatal vitamins?"

Carla nodded. "Maybe that's why this kid has been jumping around inside me like a Mexican hat dancer. Do either of you have any Mexican blood?"

"African and Scandinavian," Michael replied.

"Scottish and Italian," Cal said.

"Well, maybe he was doing a tribal dance and the tarantella." Carla flicked back her long dark hair. "While I was lying awake in bed, I did the baby's astrology and numerology charts."

Michael asked, "How can you do that without knowing his birthdate?"

Carla glared at him. "I decided if he doesn't come out of me by the end of the week, I'm pulling my nephew out with tongs."

"What did the charts show?" Cal didn't believe in the occult, but he was thankful to get Carla's mind off her discomfort.

Carla smiled. "He's going to be kind, strong, fair, honest, and quite successful."

"Of course he is. He's our son." Cal kissed Michael's cheek.

"Let's hope he's kind enough to make an appearance soon." Carla ate more of her breakfast.

Michael asked, "How is Dotty doing running the restaurant during your maternity leave?"

"Fine." Carla sat back. "I should never go back."

Cal grinned. "You wouldn't leave Carla's."

"You're right." She winked at Cal. "That restaurant is as much a part of me as Cozzi Cove is a part of you."

A month ago, complaining more than a right-wing politician at a Planned Parenthood meeting, Carla had moved into Bungalow One so that Cal and Michael could help take care of her. She had also insisted that she wanted to have their baby at Cozzi Cove, assisted by a midwife, and not in a hospital. It had seemed the perfect solution; however, since sound carried between the two bungalows, it meant inadvertently sharing their more intimate moments.

Michael seemed miles away.

"What's wrong?" Cal asked.

Michael shrugged, his head hanging down.

Carla said, "Don't be shy, Michael. You know I'm family now. I married Cal's sister. Remember? You were there, marrying this guy."

Since Michael wasn't talking, Cal asked Carla, "When *is* my dear sister coming for a visit?"

Carla sighed. "Taylor said she'd be here after her business meetings in Paris and Rome, but before her meetings in Washington, DC and New York."

"What does that mean?" Cal asked.

"It means Taylor and the conservative big-money boys are making sure the top one percent stay that way." She turned to Michael. "You're not off the hook so easily about your pouting. What's up?"

"A lot, last night." Michael patted Cal's crotch.

Cal put his arm around his husband. "We know something's wrong, Michael. Spill it."

"And feel free to spill my milk while you're at it," Carla said, pushing away her glass.

Michael pushed it back in front of her. "I wasn't going to say anything."

"But?" Cal asked.

Michael rested his chin on his hand. "Cozzi Cove has been in your family for generations, like Carla's Seafood Restaurant has been in Carla's."

"So?" Cal asked again.

"So you both belong here. I'm just a guy who fell in love with the man I tried to gay bash."

Cal took his hand. "Michael, you're my husband. Cozzi Cove is as much your home as it is mine."

"It doesn't feel that way."

Carla groaned. "Did my wife say something obnoxious to you the last time she visited?"

"Taylor said lots of obnoxious things to me the last time she visited, but that's not it."

"Then what *is* it, Michael?" Cal asked.

Michael bit his lower lip. "I love you more than I've ever loved anyone. And I can't think of a place I'd like living more than Cozzi Cove. But this is your land, your inheritance, and your soul. Sometimes I feel like an outsider."

At that moment, there was a knock at the front door. "That must be my new houseboy," Cal said, getting to his feet.

Carla leaned on the table and pushed herself off the chair. "I don't want anyone seeing me like this. I'm going back to my bungalow."

"Take this for the road," Michael said, handing her the glass of milk.

She downed the milk in one gulp and cringed. "If I don't come out of my bungalow in a week's time, send in the bulldozer." Carla left out the back kitchen door.

Cal paused at the kitchen entry, looking on as Michael cleared the table and started stacking the dishwasher. "We'll talk about this later," he said.

"It's fine, really."

Unconvinced, Cal left for the living room.

A tall young man with golden blond hair stood in the center of the room. He wore shorts that barely contained his muscular thighs, and a pink polo shirt that barely housed his massive pectoral muscles.

"The sign out front said to enter," he said with a discernable Southern accent.

"This is the first day of our summer season." Cal offered his hand. "Cal Cozzi."

The young man's biceps expanded like melons as he nearly broke the bones in Cal's hand with his firm handshake. "I'm Billy Dean Boyd."

"Where you from, Billy?"

"It's Billy Dean ever since I can remember. I'm from Mobile, Alabama."

Cal moved behind his desk. "What brings you to New Jersey, Billy Dean?"

"I was looking for a college near New York City. I'm studying theater."

Cal smiled at Billy Dean's pronunciation of "thee-aye-ter."

"But I'm here on a football scholarship."

Looking at the boy, Cal wasn't surprised. "I played football professionally."

"I know. I looked you up on the web."

"I'm surprised you found anything. My career was short and uneventful."

"My high school coach back in Mobile used to say, 'It takes a whole team to play a game.'"

"So you said you're playing football at college?"

Billy Dean nodded. "But that doesn't mean my grades aren't good. I got straight A's back in high school, and my IQ is one hundred and twenty-one."

Cal was impressed. "How did you hear about the job?"

"I saw the advertisement on a bulletin board at State."

Cal sat behind his desk and motioned for Billy Dean to take a nearby armchair. "Why do you want to be a houseboy at Cozzi Cove?"

"My mama and daddy rent out rooms back home. I've been cleaning commodes, making up beds, and fetching towels since I was a kid."

"You'll need to be here mornings to clean the bungalows and bring fresh towels. Then back again at four in the afternoon for turndown service. Will that work for you?"

"It sure will. I don't have classes or football practice yet. I'm staying at my dorm since I'm in a play at the college, but we rehearse in the evenings. Except on Wednesday nights when I have Bible study, and Friday nights are prayer meetings, and Sunday nights are services."

Cal chose his words carefully. "You know this is a gay resort?"

Billy Dean nodded and his golden locks bounced against his head. "I'm gay. That's another reason this job fits me like biscuits to gravy."

"And that doesn't interfere with your religious beliefs?"

"No, sir. I'm a red-letter Christian."

"A red-letter Christian?"

"Everything Jesus said is written in red in most Bibles. Red-letter Christians only believe those passages. Thomas Jefferson wrote his own Bible with those spiritual words of wisdom. Jesus never said anything against homosexuals. As a matter of fact, anybody who said anything bad about anybody who was different was tore slap up by Jesus."

Cal sat back in his chair, envisioning Billy Dean leaving religious tracts on pillows and proselytizing to guests.

"Don't worry," Billy Dean said, as if he could read Cal's mind. "I accepted Jesus as my Lord and personal Savior, and He lives in my heart every day, but I'd never tell y'all what to believe or not believe."

"That's good."

Billy Dean slid forward in his chair. "There is one thing you should know about me, though." He took a card out of his wallet. "This is my chastity card. I pledged back at my home church to be celibate until marriage."

Cal smiled at how different Billy Dean was from Connor, the previous houseboy. "That won't be a problem."

Billy Dean returned the smile. "Good. Jesus is the only man in my heart."

Given Cozzi Cove's aura of romance and Billy Dean's good looks, Cal assumed that would change quickly.

"The other kids in my play rush out after rehearsals and meet in their dorm rooms to get all hot and heavy. My grampa back home would tell me I'm 'nuttier than peanut brittle' for not joining them."

Cal asked, "What play are you doing?"

"*Li'l Abner*. I'm the lead."

Given Billy Dean's good looks, strapping build, irresistible charm, and Southern accent, Cal wasn't surprised. He got an honest vibe from the boy, and he was excited about the possibility of Billy Dean unloading the supply truck when it made deliveries to Cozzi Cove.

"To get us started, I cleaned, aired out, and put fresh linens, towels, and bathroom supplies in all the bungalows. Michael mowed the lawns, watered the plants, and cleaned out the hot tub in each one."

"That's me," Michael said as he entered the room.

"Michael's my husband," Cal explained.

"I just graduated from State," Michael added.

Billy Dean sat and stared at them blankly.

After a few moments, Cal asked, "Is there something wrong? Billy Dean?"

Billy Dean came to like a healed coma victim. "Did I fall asleep with my eyes open?"

"I'm not sure," Cal replied.

"I probably did. I have narcolepsy. Since I was a kid. I doze off briefly without realizing it. Sometimes with my eyes open. Sometimes with them closed. Y'all will get used to it."

Cal asked, "Isn't it dangerous for you to drive?"

"I ride a bicycle."

"How do you play football and act in plays?" Michael asked, clearly having overheard Billy Dean's interview with Cal.

"It generally doesn't happen when my adrenaline is high, or right after I take my medicine," Billy Dean explained.

Cal and Michael shared a concerned look.

"It won't interfere with my duties here," he said quickly. "Something else my grampa would tell you is that I work faster than a termite in an old building.'"

Cal smiled. "I really like your expressions, Billy Dean."

"Thank my grampa. He's the best. I really miss him." Billy Dean smiled. "How about this one? 'I'll work harder than a bull with his butt on fire in a pepper patch.'"

The three of them laughed. Cal looked into the boy's crystal-blue eyes and trusted him. "When can you start?"

"Do I have the job?" Billy Dean asked.

Cal looked at Michael who nodded his approval. "Let's give it a try."

"Praise the Lord!" Billy Dean said, smiling from ear to ear.

"I probably wouldn't say that around here," Michael offered.

"I understand." Billy Dean shook both of their hands happily. "I can start right now if you like."

Cal turned to Michael. "Can you show Billy Dean around the supply room and the bungalows, and go over his duties?"

"Sure," Michael replied.

Cal faced Billy Dean. "Then take some time for lunch, and come back at four o'clock for turndown service. You get paid every Friday the rate on the ad. Any questions?"

"Can I use a bathroom in one of the bungalows?" Billy Dean asked.

"As long as you clean it afterward," Cal replied.

Michael headed to the front porch. "Follow me, Billy Dean."

Cal turned on his computer and answered his e-mail messages, hoping the summer would bring lots of business to Cozzi Cove. His sister had been on his back for years, trying to convince him to sell Cozzi Cove or turn it into condos. He knew deep in his heart that business would pick up. Now, what was in his heart needed to turn into financial reality.

Looking up, Cal saw a handsome, brawny, dark-skinned man enter through the front door. He looked to be about thirty, was dressed in a tan jacket and dress pants, and carried a leather travel bag.

"Welcome to Cozzi Cove," Cal said.

"This place is amazing. The view at the cove is obscenely beautiful."

"No arguments here."

The man unveiled a row of straight white teeth. "I'm Nijad Hadad. I'm a travel agent, but I haven't seen many places as nice as this. And it has a magical feel about it."

"That's what everyone says who stays here." Cal examined his computer screen. "I have your credit card information." He handed Nijad the key and map. "You're in Bungalow Five."

A tall, pale man about Nijad's age entered the living room behind Nijad. His baby blue dress shirt and slacks hung loosely on his thin frame. His blond hair fell over his marine-blue eyes.

"Is this the front office?"

Cal smiled. "And my home. I'm Cal Cozzi. Are you staying with us this week?"

The man nodded and placed his bag at his feet. "I'm Andrew Urban." He added, "My sister, Annabel, will be joining me."

Cal punched a few keys on his computer keyboard. "You are in Bungalow Six."

"Right next door to me. Hello, I'm Nijad Hadad."

The men locked eyes and shook hands. They lingered a bit longer than normal before releasing.

Cal gave Andrew his key and map, and then spoke to both men. "Feel free to use the cove whenever you like, as well as the public beach only a mile away. Your cars are fine in our parking lot, and there's also a lot at the main beach. The map will show you the town park, grocery store, bookstore, diner, Carla's Seafood Restaurant, Tommy Malone's bar, the miniature golf center, the trampoline emporium, and the saltwater taffy shop."

"I won't want to go home." Nijad smiled at Andrew.

Andrew returned the smile.

"Where is home for you and your sister?" Nijad asked with a hopeful gaze.

"Jersey City. But Cozzi Cove is home for the next week," Andrew replied.

Nijad said, "I live in Paramus. But I'll be at Cozzi Cove all week."

They both looked relieved.

Nijad asked, "What do you do for a living?"

"I'm a flight attendant."

"And your sister?"

"She's a flight attendant too."

"I'm a travel agent. We have a lot in common."

They shared another smile.

"My staff are busy at present, so I'll show you to your bungalows." Cal put the Be Right Back sign on the porch door and led the two men outside.

As they walked past the other bungalows, the men gazed at the translucent bay water dancing up toward the soft blue sky.

"I've been to many places. Few can compare to this," Andrew said.

Nijad laughed. "I told Cal the same thing."

Andrew giggled. "We think alike."

"It appears so."

Cal thought Cozzi Cove wouldn't have to work its romantic magic too hard to bring these two together. He opened the door to Bungalow Five. "This is your bungalow, Nijad. Would you like help with your bag?"

"I can manage."

Cal said, "The kitchen is in the back of the bungalow complete with all kitchen appliances, pots, pans, dishware, and utensils. Do you have any questions?"

"Just one." Nijad looked at Andrew. "I hope this isn't too forward. In my line of work, we can be somewhat blunt. I don't want to offend you."

"What is it?" Andrew asked.

"Would you consider joining me for dinner at Carla's Seafood Restaurant this evening?"

After a few beats, Andrew replied, "Yes. I'd like that."

"Will your sister mind?" Nijad asked.

"No. I'm not even sure when she'll be getting in."

"May I knock on your bungalow door at seven?"

"That will be fine."

Nijad nodded happily and closed the bungalow door behind him.

Cal led Andrew to his bungalow next door, opened the door, and led Andrew inside. He rested Andrew's bag on the stand in the front bedroom. "There's also a back bedroom for your sister. You already heard my bit about the kitchen. The bathroom is also stocked with supplies, and the hot tub in the backyard turns on by a flick of the red button. The black dial sets the temperature." Cal thought it might come in handy, no pun intended, after Andrew's dinner date with Nijad. "Don't hesitate to call the front desk if you need anything."

Andrew smiled in obvious anticipation of his evening. "I think I have everything I need."

Cal returned to the main bungalow to find a bald, more than middle-aged man in Bermuda shorts and a Hawaiian shirt standing at the front door reading a brochure labeled, "Convention of Horrors." Sitting quietly at his feet was a reddish-brown Irish setter.

"Hello. Sorry I was away from my desk. Please come in." Cal led the small, thin man through the front porch and into the living room. The dog followed obediently. "I'm Cal Cozzi."

"Jonathan Harper. Tax auditor. But don't panic. I'm not here for an audit."

"Looks like you're here for the horror convention in the next town."

Jonathan nodded and set his bag down. "I've loved horror movies, TV shows, and books since I was a kid. My parents used to worry that I'd have nightmares. But it was quite the opposite. A haunted house, a vengeful ghost, a thirsty vampire, or a twisted werewolf only lulled me to sleep each night. Even as a teenager, I thought vampires were sexy. When the heroines in those old movies wore garlic necklaces and carried wooden stakes, I always thought, 'What's wrong with you, honey?' If a handsome man with slicked back black hair, broad shoulders, and a flowing cape had wanted to suck on my neck, I'd have declared it open season for a transfusion."

Cal was thankful for his "normal" childhood. "You're in Bungalow Three, Jonathan. Here are your key and map of the town. Feel free to use the cove, the main beach—"

"I'll be busy at the convention for most of the week."

Given Jonathan's eccentricities, Cal was grateful for that. "Your dog is welcome to stay in the bungalow or explore the cove if you're with him." He handed Jonathan the rules and policies for pets. "Please read and sign this."

Jonathan did as Cal asked. Then he spoke to the dog. "You hear that, Renfield?"

The dog stood up at attention.

Jonathan explained to Cal, "Renfield is a character in Bram Stoker's *Dracula*. He was a patient in an insane asylum who ate insects to drain and utilize their life force." He turned to the dog. "Renfield, say hello to Cal."

Renfield raised his paw, and Cal shook it. Cal said, "Nice dog."

"He loves going to cemeteries with me." Jonathan petted Renfield's head, and then Renfield licked Jonathan's hand.

"Please follow me." Cal led his latest guest along the cove and into his bungalow. As he placed Jonathan's bag in the front bedroom, Renfield sat next to his owner and rested his head on his shoe. Cal said, "There's a view of the cove from these windows, the living room windows, and the front porch of course."

"Does the moon rise over the bay at night?" Jonathan asked with a twinkle in his dark eyes.

"It sure does."

Jonathan sat on the king-sized four-poster with his legs dangling over the side. Renfield jumped up onto the bed next to him. "I read online that your great-grandfather built this place."

"And most of the town of Cozzi. Hence the name."

"Has anyone ever seen his ghost here?"

Cal peeked at his watch. "Not that I know of."

Jonathan petted Renfield. "Since he built this place, your great-grandfather's spirit must visit it sometime."

"I wouldn't know about that."

Renfield rolled over and Jonathan rubbed his tummy. "Ghosts visit in various ways."

"I'll let you know if I ever hear from him."

"I have a feeling you'll be hearing from him soon."

"Have a nice stay."

Cal headed back to the main bungalow, and took the sign off the front door. He then passed through the front porch to his office, where he found a tall, gym-bodied, dark-skinned man waiting for him. The man was wearing a royal-blue pinstriped designer suit and expensive-looking gold jewelry. There was something Cal found familiar about him, but he couldn't place what it was.

Moving behind his desk, Cal asked, "Can I help you?"

The man placed his designer luggage on the floor. "I'm Malcolm Wolf."

Cal checked his computer screen. "Yes, Mr. Wolf from New York."

"I also have a place in LA."

Cal thought the guy was a bit full of himself. "You're in Bungalow Two." He handed him the key and map. "You are free to use the cove—"

"I know."

Cal looked at him inquisitively. "Have you stayed with us before?"

"Actually, I worked here for your dad—as a houseboy. I lived with my mother a few towns away. The money helped put me through college."

"I thought you looked familiar." Cal took in the strapping man. "But I wasn't sure."

He laughed. "I was skinny as a string bean back then."

"How long did you work here?"

"When I was eighteen and nineteen and attending the community college. You were in high school. The young lord of the manor back then."

Cal couldn't help but detect a sarcastic tone. "I apologize for not recognizing you."

"Your dad used to call me Big Mac."

Cal envisioned a tall, thin, and lanky college kid hurrying around Cozzi Cove, often asking him how his day went at school. "I remember now. Why did you leave us?"

"I got a scholarship to Yale."

"Good for you. What do you do now?"

"I started out as a newspaper copy editor. Now I'm senior editor for a magazine."

Michael entered the room as Malcolm stated the name of his magazine, one of the biggest in the country.

Cal rose and put his arm around Michael. "Malcolm Wolf, this is Michael Rodgers, my husband. Michael recently graduated from the state college with a degree in photojournalism."

Malcolm revealed a porcelain-veneered white smile. "Congratulations, Michael."

"Malcolm used to work for my dad. Now he's the senior editor of a big magazine." Cal hoped Michael would catch the bait and ask Malcolm for a job.

As Michael stood there dumbstruck, Cal said, "Michael, has Billy Dean gone home?"

Michael nodded, still staring at Malcolm.

"Will you do me a favor and show Malcolm to Bungalow Two?" Cal asked with a nudging gaze.

Slowly taking Malcolm's bag, Michael said, "Come to job. I mean, please come with me."

Cal breathed a sigh of relief as Michael led Malcolm out the front door without banging into it.

* * *

Michael Rodgers' mouth was dry, his eyes were wet, and his mind was vacant. He had been trying for months to get an interview with someone like Malcolm Wolf, and here stood the magazine editor right in his own backyard, or bungalow. Bungalow Two to be precise. Michael opened the door and led Malcolm through the glass-enclosed porch and into the front bedroom.

After carefully placing the designer luggage on the stand, Michael said, "I like your job, I mean your suit."

"Thanks." Malcolm reached into his wallet for a tip.

"No, thank you."

"All right." Malcolm put his wallet back inside his pocket. "What was your subject matter?"

"My subject matter?" Michael swallowed hard.

"What articles have you done?" Malcolm sat in the chair at the desk.

Over his knocking knees and grinding stomach, Michael shouted, "One was about LGBV people toting." He realized what he'd said. "I mean LGBT people voting."

"I knew what you meant." Malcolm gestured for Michael to sit on the bed.

Michael complied and said, "It was for a gay magazine called—"

"There's a problem right there."

"A problem?"

Malcolm nodded. "You don't want to pigeonhole yourself into working on articles for gays, blacks, or young people. Mainstream is where the money, audience, and prestige are."

"But I am gay, black, and young. People like me buy magazines." Michael thought, *This must have been what it was like for the Cowardly Lion finding his courage.*

"Only if they're online."

"Isn't your magazine also online?"

"Sure. We have an online presence as well." Malcolm came from behind the desk to sit next to Michael. "Let me explain what I mean. There's nothing wrong with being young. I was young once. Obviously, I'm a black man. And though I'm married to a lovely, intelligent, cultured woman who makes me proud at business functions, my sexuality is fluid. Something I'd like to keep between us."

Michael had heard about black men "on the down-low." Though he himself had struggled with coming out, the idea of marrying a woman and being secretly gay always struck him as being untruthful.

"I was brought up to believe in the Bible, and that marriage is only between one man and one woman. But Cal and his family and friends helped me realize we're all created as we are, and nobody is evil, especially people in love. Using books written thousands of years ago to stifle women, blacks, or gays is no longer godly to me."

"I'm not talking about the Bible, Michael."

"Then what are you talking about?"

Malcolm scratched at his designer haircut. "Power."

"Power?"

Malcolm nodded. "Black people don't have it. Neither do young people. Gay people certainly don't have it."

"There are some powerful gay political organizations."

"Let me ask you something. Do you think it's powerful to allow conservative politicians to pass laws saying you don't have the same rights as they do? To make campaign speeches saying you don't matter? That you're against God, nature, the family, and the country?"

"No."

"Then why do you want to work for a weak, powerless group who accepts that?"

Michael didn't know what to say.

"You want to take photos for the people with the power."

"Who's that?"

"White, straight, Christian, wealthy men. If you want to have power, you need to work for *them*."

Michael couldn't help thinking how well Malcolm would get along with Cal's sister who was a financial investor for the rich and famous. "But there's also a market for other audiences."

"A niche market."

"What's wrong with that?"

"Nothing. If you want to make very little money and have your work seen by very few people." Malcolm rested his hand on Michael's shoulder. "Look, how about you bring over your article tomorrow. I'll take a look at it and see if I think you have the talent to move up to the mainstream."

"Wow! Thank you," Michael said as if he'd won the lottery. He got up and strode to the bedroom doorway. "Mr. Wolf, I'm not complaining, but why are you doing this for me? I'm a nobody, and you're at the top of your field."

"It's Malcolm. And I made that offer because you remind me a great deal of myself when I was your age. I was from this area, ready to change the world. Take journalism by storm. Let's look at this as one brother helping another brother." Malcolm rose and came face to face with Michael. "Do we have a deal?"

"We sure do."

Malcolm shook his hand and then held it. "I look forward to seeing you tomorrow, Michael."

Michael nodded and left the bungalow as if walking on air.

CHAPTER TWO

That evening, Cal finished loading the dishwasher with the dinner dishes and walked Carla back to her bungalow. When he returned home, he found himself standing in the front bedroom, missing Michael who was working at Tommy's bar. Cal slipped out of his shorts and sandals and went over to the bookcase to scan the dozens of "how to raise a baby" books he and Michael had been reading over the last six months. Feeling pangs of nervousness about his upcoming fatherhood, Cal reached for one of the books, which slipped out of his hand and fell against the baseboard molding. Bending down to pick up the book, Cal noticed the molding had come loose. He groaned at the thought of having to repair it. Upon closer inspection, he saw a thin black leather book lodged between the molding and the wall. His brother hadn't touched the original molding when doing the renovations, and Cal assumed by the faded leather cover that the book had been there for many years. He reached in and carefully lifted it without tearing the frayed edges. Then Cal brought the book to bed, lay down on his stomach, and opened to the first page.

This is the diary of Calvin Cozzi.

Cal's father never mentioned keeping a diary. Then Cal noticed the first entry date:

June 1, 1937. It was his great-grandfather's diary! Cal proceeded to read the first entry.

My name is Calvin Cozzi. I am thirty years old. I live in a town named after my father, Cozzi, in New Jersey on the seashore. We are not that far away from where the German ship Hindenburg went up in flames in May. I have never written a diary before. I guess I never saw the need. But lately, I have had some thoughts going around in my head that I cannot share with anyone else. I hope writing them down in this journal will help me make some sense of them.

I am tall with auburn hair and green eyes. Everyone says I am a strapping man. That is probably because I worked in the steel mill with my father, until the strike, and until my father, Franklin Cozzi, passed away from tuberculosis. My wife died in childbirth a year ago. So now it is just my mother, my baby Calvin Cozzi Jr., and me living in this two-bedroom house that my father built in the center of town. My mama is bathing the baby in the kitchen sink. I am writing this at my desk next to the fireplace in my bedroom, which I share with the baby.

I just noticed a hole in my breeches, the soles of my boots are wearing thin, and my cap brim is sagging. Things have been rough since the stock market crash back in 1929. President Roosevelt is doing the best he can. I heard he is thinking up some kind of new deal to get people back to work. I sure hope so, since they said on the radio that seven million people in our country are out of work. Nobody is building much of anything right now since a new house costs as much as four thousand dollars! So carpenters are out of work too. Even some college fellows are unemployed unless they are a lawyer, doctor, or accountant. Our old Ford growls and sputters, but with a car costing about seven hundred dollars now, I will not be getting a new one. We do not go out a great deal anyway since gas is as much as ten cents a gallon! Mama watches every penny at the grocery store with bread going for nine cents a loaf.

I love my family dearly, but maybe it would be better if I went away someplace. What good am I to anyone here? I'm unemployed and grumpy all the time. The baby is up crying most of the night. I try my best, but nothing I do calms him down. Mama holds him, and he stops crying right away.

Before he passed, my father won a strip of land in a poker game at Malone's saloon. It is a pretty cove about a mile away from the beach. Over the years, softer rocks were worn away by the sun and salty water quicker than the harder rocks around them. This formed a bay of turquoise water surrounded by large rocks in the distance and smaller rocks near the white sand. The lighthouse in the distance warns boats they are heading for the cove.

My passion is going to the main beach and swimming in the ocean. I like looking up at the clear blue sky while I swim through the cold foamy water. Then I head over to my daddy's cove and lay out on the warm white sand, breathe in the salty air, and listen to the sound of the seagulls and the waves tickling the rocks. That is when I start to think about my secret. Maybe someday I will have the nerve to tell you about it, diary.

The baby is crying again. Mama just came in to feed him. I better go. Until next time. Yours truly, Calvin Cozzi.

Cal couldn't believe what he was reading. Jonathan Harper had been right about Cal hearing from his great-grandfather. He read the next entry.

June 3, 1937.

Sorry I did not write yesterday. The baby was sick, and I had to go fetch Doc Robinson. Calvin Jr. is better now. Mama is with him. I am back at my desk in my bedroom, looking at the books in my bookcase. Of Mice and Men reminds me of our bad economic times. The Adventures of Tom Sawyer and Huckleberry Finn cause me to miss the adventures I had as a boy, running through the woods, making a raft out of an old tire for the beach, and listening to my father tell stories about when he was a boy. Lost Horizon and its tale of Shangri-La makes me think back to the tree house my father and I built in the backyard. As I stare at those books, I think about the strip of land at the cove, and an idea forms in my head. Lots of people like going to the beach. What if I built a bungalow for my family and seven other bungalows to rent out in the summer? Seven for seven days of the week. I can make the furniture with a nautical theme, like end tables and bed headboards in the shape of boats, desks in the shape of fish, and lighting fixtures with carvings of seashells and mermaids. I can do the construction myself with the help of an assistant, who will hopefully work for room and board, living in our attic. My credit is good in town. So I can take out a loan for supplies with my old school chum Tucker Fredericks at the bank. Suddenly, I feel alive again, laughing in delight at the excitement of new possibilities. I am going to build and manage a resort on the bay. And I am going to call it Cozzi Cove.

Cal got out of bed and went to stand at the bedroom window. He gazed out at the cove, thinking about his great-grandfather.

* * *

Nijad Hadad stepped out of Bungalow Five onto the cove, wearing an olive blazer and slacks that matched his skin tone. He had combed his thick jet-black hair off his forehead, and had some difficulty getting his jacket over his gym body. He was anxious for his date with Andrew Urban, so he had already looked in his dresser mirror for any stray hairs in his prominent nose, any hidden food particles in his large white teeth, or any red lines in the whites of his dark eyes. At the front door of Bungalow Six, Nijad sniffed under his arms, checked his breath in his cupped hands, and glanced down to make sure his fly wasn't open. Satisfied with all three queries, he knocked on the door.

Andrew opened the door wearing white slacks and a powder-blue dress shirt that matched his eyes perfectly. His soft blond hair framed his porcelain-like skin.

A warm smile graced his handsome face. "Nijad, please come in."

As he followed Andrew from the porch past the front bedroom to the living room, Nijad said, "Your bungalow is just like mine." He peeked into the back bedroom and laughed at the sight of women's clothes, makeup products, handbags, and toiletries all over the bed, bureau, and desk. "Your sister's, I presume?"

"Yes. Annabel got in an hour ago."

"Where is she?"

"At the beauty salon getting her hair done."

"With all those grooming products, the stylist should come *here*." When Andrew laughed at his joke, Nijad relaxed. He liked a man with a good sense of humor.

"Would you like a drink?" Andrew asked. "I went into town and bought wine, beer, milk, juice, and bottled water. I don't drink alcohol."

Nijad didn't need alcohol to have a good evening with a handsome man. "Water is fine."

A few moments later, Nijad and Andrew were seated on the glider on the front porch with bottled water in their hands. Nijad looked out at the cove. "I love this time of day, before the sun sets."

Andrew nodded. "Me too."

"It's so peaceful and calm. And the color of the sky matches your eyes," Nijad said. "It's beautiful."

Andrew smiled. "Thank you. The bay water is relaxing. And the rocks are like works of art. Cozzi Cove is a hidden gem."

"You must travel a great deal," Nijad said, drawn to Andrew's shy but sophisticated manner and unable to take his eyes off his square shoulders and warm face.

"That's the lot of a flight attendant."

"Where is your favorite place?"

Andrew sighed. "Ireland is magical with gorgeous green mountains resting over blue waters. Italy's cities offer a different type of beauty, from the art in Florence to the history in Rome to the canals of Venice. Paris is so romantic with its balconied buildings, and the French countryside is breathtaking. London is an amazing cultural city, and nearby are the Cotswold storybook villages. I could go on and on."

"Did you go to college?"

Andrew nodded. "The local state school."

"So did I. And your sister?"

"Annabel went to university in Kent."

"Did she like it?"

"She must have since she stayed there nine more years, coming back occasionally to visit me."

"When did she return here to live?"

"Just last year. Are you trying to figure out my age?"

"Tell me the difference in yours and Annabel's ages and I'll be successful."

"None." Andrew smiled. "We're twins."

"Ah! Is it true that twins always know what the other is thinking?"

"Most of the time, yes. Annabel and I were extremely close as children. We played together for hours on end, mostly sneaking dolls into our bedroom and dressing them. We read the same books, liked the same TV shows. We were inseparable."

"I'm looking forward to meeting her."

"You probably will."

"But right now, I'm more interested in Annabel's brother." Nijad moved closer to Andrew and enjoyed the sensation. "How is it that someone your age who has traveled all over the world is unattached?" He smiled. "And yes, I am trying to find out if you're single."

Andrew rested back in the love seat. "I've dated a number of men, but it never worked out."

"Why is that?"

"I don't think they understood me."

"Are you so difficult to understand?"

"Extremely."

Nijad winked. "Ah, a man of mystery."

"And how about you?" Andrew asked. "As a travel agent you must have seen the world. How is it that nobody's caught you yet?"

"People tend to flee when they get to know all about me."

"Hm, another man of mystery."

"We will have to uncover each other's secrets."

"To solving mysteries."

They toasted with their water bottles.

Shortly afterward, they drove in Nijad's sports car to Carla's Seafood Restaurant. Nijad parked the car, and they headed into the restaurant known for its nautical décor that included models of anchors, buoys, lighthouses, and sailboats. Dotty, a pretty young woman, greeted them at the door and sat them at a table next to the fireplace. After ordering their main courses, they enjoyed mouthwatering spicy shrimp marinara appetizers.

Nijad couldn't help himself; he had to say it: "You look amazing in the candlelight."

"Thank you. You look very nice too."

There was something wholesome, warm, and friendly about Andrew. "I'm usually not this forward the first day I meet someone."

Andrew batted his eyelashes. "What are you usually like?"

"Believe it or not, shy."

"Me too. I didn't have many friends growing up."

"But you had your sister."

Andrew nodded. "Our mother was...not very well, and our father wasn't home a lot."

"I'm sorry to hear that," Nijad replied. "Are your parents still alive?"

"My father passed away. He was a lawyer. My mother lives on fake disability claims."

Nijad wanted to hold Andrew in his arms and tell him everything would be all right. Instead, he nodded his sympathy.

"How about you?" Andrew asked.

"My parents are from Libya. My father is a doctor, and my mother is a nurse. They moved to the States before I was born."

"Lucky for you, given the anti-gay laws in so many countries in the Middle East."

Nijad sobered quickly. "It's tragic how many people there use the Koran to keep women as property and gays hidden in the shadows." He swallowed hard.

"Have you ever been there?"

Nijad shook his head. "Gay men there live under cover in fear of being found, imprisoned, raped, and even killed. I'd love to see the land of my family, but I don't want to risk it. My parents have never gone back."

The waiter served their entrees—maple salmon for Nijad and lobster-stuffed sole for Andrew.

Andrew dug into a brussels sprout, and a piece of it landed on his chin. Nijad wiped it off, and they shared a smile. "Do you have any siblings?"

"Two brothers. One joined the Navy, and the other moved to California," Nijad replied.

"Now I know why you are staying at Cozzi Cove. The love of water seems to be in your family."

Nijad swallowed his delicious bite of sweet salmon and moved on to taste the creamy garlic mashed potatoes. "Why are *you* staying here?"

"I found Cozzi Cove on the Web. It reminded me of a cove I visited near the Canterbury River in Kent."

Their gazes connected.

"Thank you for having dinner with me. I hope we can see more of each other this week at Cozzi Cove." Nijad took a leap. "And perhaps afterward."

"I'd like that."

When they had finished their dinners and were eating Carla's pumpkin cheesecake with pumpkin spice herbal tea, Nijad decided it was time. "As I mentioned back in your bungalow, there's something about me you don't know."

"I'm sure there are a great many things about you I don't know and vice versa." Andrew flashed his perfectly straight white teeth.

"I'd like to start to rectify that."

"Please do." Andrew gestured for Nijad to continue.

"I'm bisexual."

"You mean you're attracted to both men and women?"

"Yes. Ever since puberty."

Andrew slid forward in his chair. "Are you a number three on the Kinsey Scale?"

"If you mean are my attractions equal to both sexes, yes. But I'm not a sexaholic, cheater, or closet gay as many people might think."

"I don't think that."

Nijad's broad shoulders relaxed. "I'm glad."

"It sounds like it has caused some difficulties for you."

Nijad nodded, not wanting to lie to Andrew. "Some people don't understand it."

A knot formed between Andrew's eyebrows. "Is one person able to fulfill you?"

"Not so far."

"Have you ever had a threesome?"

"No. I'm not interested in that." Nijad wanted Andrew to understand. "I'd like to have a strong relationship with one person."

"But so far that hasn't been possible?"

Nijad nodded.

"Thank you for sharing that with me. As a gay man, it's not my reality, and I appreciate you explaining it to me."

"As a gay man, you don't need to be intimate with every man you're attracted to," Nijad said.

Andrew laughed. "I'd be pretty busy if I were."

"It's the same with me being attracted to people of both sexes."

"Do you think you'll have a happily-ever-after ending?"

Nijad took in Andrew. "I hope so."

They finished their desserts, left Carla's, and drove back to Cozzi Cove. After parking in the lot, they strolled down the cove, lit only by moonlight and with only the sound of bay water gently lapping against the rocks. When they arrived at the door to Bungalow Six, Nijad said, "I had a wonderful time."

"Me too." Andrew unleashed his captivating smile.

"I feel as though we talked about me for most of the night. I'd like to get together again and find out more about you."

Andrew grinned like a child with a secret. "I'm playing miniature golf in town tomorrow."

"Do you enjoy that?"

"Not really. Annabel loves it. Would you like to come?"

Nijad found Andrew's giddiness infectious. "I'd love to."

"Great. Come meet me at my bungalow at one."

"I will."

They stared into each other's eyes. Not wanting to break the contact and again unable to stop himself, Nijad wrapped his arms around Andrew, leaned in, and kissed him softly on the lips. Andrew smelled of ginger and oranges. To Nijad's excitement, Andrew returned the embrace. They kissed again and again and again. Nijad didn't want to stop.

Andrew broke away. "Thank you for a terrific evening, Nijad. I'm looking forward to tomorrow." He went into the bungalow and shut the door after him.

Nijad headed for the bungalow next door, floating on a cloud. He gazed out at the old lighthouse, now a charcoal silhouette in the distance, and he laughed at how love at first sight was for hopeless romantics. As he opened his bungalow door, he couldn't deny being pretty hopelessly and incredibly romantic.

* * *

Jonathan Harper made his way down the cove, nodded at the Middle Eastern man going into his bungalow, and let himself into Bungalow Three. He had spent most of the afternoon and early evening at the local Horror Convention getting autographs from has-been stars of long-ago cancelled television shows that had featured ghosts, vampires, werewolves, witches, and warlocks. He had also collected brochures about upcoming movies, television shows, and web series with occult themes. Finally, after purchasing as many books on the occult as he could carry, he'd listened to pitches from salespeople peddling vampire fangs and capes, werewolf masks, ghost hunter costumes, witches' books of spells and caldrons, blood mouthwash, no-reflection mirrors, and specialty coffins and gravestones.

Exhausted, Jonathan unloaded his purchases onto the desk in the front bedroom and dragged himself into the kitchen where he ate the dinner he'd brought back from the convention: "bloody" chicken fingers (with ketchup), "poisonous" herbed potatoes, and onion "eyes."

Then, sitting on the front porch with his dog Renfield at his feet, Jonathan rested back on the rocking chair and bathed in the moonlight. He heard a howling in the distance and assumed it was a stray dog. When Renfield's ears pricked up and he whimpered, Jonathan thought perhaps it wasn't just a dog. He petted Renfield as he rocked back and forth, both of them listening attentively to every sound in the night.

Jonathan gasped at the glimpse of a flowing cape a ways off. He craned his neck to see more, but it was too dark. He got up, with Renfield following close behind, opened the front door, and ventured out onto the cove. Standing on the white sand for several moments, Jonathan couldn't make anything out in the dusk. Just as he was about to go back into his bungalow, Renfield froze, mesmerized by something. Jonathan followed Renfield's fixed gaze to a tall, slender figure in a black suit and cape that seemed to be from another time and place. The man appeared to be about fifty, with features chiseled into his handsome face and black hair flowing nearly to his shoulders. While the moonlight cast a shadow behind Jonathan, it had no such effect on the man who was partially hidden behind a tall rock. As Jonathan and Renfield continued to stare, the man spun his cape.

"Who are you?" Jonathan called out sharply.

The man's voice was deep and penetrating. "I am Count Dracula."

Jonathan gasped in delight. "Are you a vampire?" Jonathan's voice quivered as much as his body.

"I am." Dracula walked around the rock and came closer to Jonathan.

He moved with incredible grace and agility. It was like a scene in a horror movie. Jonathan asked, "Are you going to bite my neck?" The thought of it was enticing.

Dracula smiled, revealing large white fangs. "Do you want me to bite your neck?"

Jonathan nodded, practically orgasmic.

Dracula grasped Jonathan's shoulders with powerful hands, pulled him close to him, and buried his fangs into Jonathan's neck.

White dots danced in front of Jonathan's eyes, and then blackness.

CHAPTER THREE

The next morning, Jonathan Harper woke up in his bed in the front bedroom of Bungalow Three having slept more soundly than he had in years. He yawned, scratched his bald head and flat stomach, and petted Renfield who lay next to him. Then he remembered the night before on the cove. Had Count Dracula really visited Cozzi Cove and bitten him? Jonathan leapt out of bed with Renfield at his heels, and hurried to the mirror on top of the bureau. Examining his neck, he found two bite marks. But he didn't look pale, or at least more pale than usual. And he wasn't weak. As a matter of fact, he was full of energy.

He heard a knock at the bungalow's front door. Still in his boxers and T-shirt, Jonathan slipped on jeans and hurried to the door with Renfield close behind. Upon opening it, Jonathan gasped and staggered backward at the sight of Count Dracula wearing a burgundy robe. Dracula's dark hypnotic gaze locked on Jonathan's. Renfield also stared at Dracula as if in a trance.

"Can I come in?" Dracula asked, shielding his face from the early morning sun.

Unable to speak, Jonathan nodded and stepped aside.

Dracula stepped into the porch with a gorgeous fluffy white dog at his side. "This is Barnabas, my Samoyed."

Barnabas sniffed Renfield who sniffed back, and they curled up side by side under the glider.

Dracula said, "Looks like Barnabas found a new friend. What's your dog's name?"

"Renfield," Jonathan squeaked, like a pubescent choirboy no longer able to hit a high note.

"Renfield led me to your bungalow last night, after you fainted."

Jonathan staggered to a rocking chair and fell into it. "Then it really happened? You bit me when we were on the cove last night?"

Dracula smiled. "You said you wanted me to."

"I did."

"Then why do you look so upset?"

"I'm not upset. Just surprised."

Dracula motioned to the other rocking chair, and, after Jonathan nodded, he took a seat next to him. "Why are you surprised?"

"I've always believed in vampires, and I love reading about them and watching movies about them, but I never thought I'd actually meet one, and be bitten by one."

Dracula laughed. "You haven't."

Jonathan did a double take. "But you just said you bit me at the cove."

"I did." He took a pair of plastic fangs out of his robe pocket. "With these."

"But what about the bite marks on my neck?"

Dracula displayed the red dye on the fangs.

Jonathan sank back in the chair. "I'm confused."

"No wonder. Where are my manners? My name's Vlad Lesti. I'm an actor hired by the convention to portray Dracula. I saw you there yesterday getting autographs from the past stars. I'm a method actor, and when we met out at the cove last night, I was doing my vampire thing, rehearsing with my cape and fangs. When you fainted in my arms, Renfield showed me the way to your bungalow. The door was unlocked, so I brought you to your bedroom and laid you down on the bed. When I asked if you were all right, you mumbled something about feeling like Lucy Westenra from *Dracula*. Since you seemed okay, I said good night and left for my bungalow next door. I'd have come earlier to see how you were doing, but I'm not a morning person by any stretch of the imagination."

Jonathan's head was reeling. "Why don't you like the sun?"

"My eyes are sensitive to bright light."

"At the cove last night, you were so strong and agile."

"Actors nowadays have to have a gym membership, take voice and dance classes, and learn how to do just about everything."

"I couldn't see your shadow."

"The large rock must have blocked it."

Jonathan grasped for a compact mirror on the end table and held it up to Vlad's face. "You don't have a reflection!"

Vlad took the mirror and examined it. "This is one of those trick mirrors they sell at the convention. You must have bought it there."

"How come you're wearing an old-fashioned burgundy robe?"

"It makes me feel like a Shakespearean actor."

"You had a power over Renfield."

"I like dogs, and they seem to sense that. As you can see, I have one of my own."

"You seem to have an answer for everything."

Vlad smiled, revealing large white molars. "Are you saying you thought I was a *real* vampire?"

"Yes."

"I'm a better actor than I thought."

Jonathan looked him up and down. "Tell me your name again?"

"Tell me yours first."

"Jonathan Harper."

"Vlad Lesti." He offered his hand.

Jonathan examined his large hand as he shook it. "It's quite cold."

"I've always had sluggish circulation."

"Where are your parents from?"

Vlad rubbed his temples. "Let's see, my mom's side of the family is from Naples, Italy, and my dad's roots are from Romania."

"Oh my God!" Jonathan clutched at his heart. "Transylvania was in the central part of Romania during the fifteenth century!"

"So?"

"Don't you see the connection?"

Vlad laughed. "I'm an actor. This week, I'm playing Dracula at the Horror Convention. Last week, I was a dancing sponge in a commercial for dish soap. The week before, I was a pickle in the parking lot of a fast-food restaurant."

Jonathan raced into the front bedroom, grabbed his laptop, and returned in a flash. "I can find the lineage site quickly," he said as he booted it up. "Tell me the name and birthplace of every one of your relatives that you know about."

"Can I shave, shower, and eat breakfast first?"

"What time do you have to be at the convention?"

"When it opens at ten thirty."

"I'll find you there."

"You'll find Dracula, my character, not Vlad the actor."

"When can I talk to you?"

"How about after the convention?"

"I'll be eating dinner."

"Okay, come to my bungalow, number four, for dinner."

Jonathan couldn't ignore his attraction to the handsome man. "All right. In the meantime, please try to remember as many of your older relatives as you can."

"Are we also going to look at *your* heritage? Jonathan Harper sounds a great deal like Jonathan Harker, the first character we meet in the *Dracula* novel." Vlad smiled. "See, I did my research."

"Jonathan Harker was English. My lineage is Irish and Scottish."

Renfield and Barnabas licked each other's necks.

Jonathan looked at Vlad suspiciously. "Why is your dog named after a famous vampire character from television?"

"Why is your dog named after the guy who ate bugs in *Dracula*?"

"This isn't about *me*. Well, maybe it is a little. I have a sixth sense about the occult."

"And your sixth sense tells you I'm a descendant of Dracula?"

Jonathan rose. "Yes."

"We can figure all that out tonight. In the meantime, I'll see you at the convention." Vlad also stood. "Remember, stay away from me." His dark eyes twinkled. "Unless you want me to bite you again."

As they walked to the front door with their dogs following, Jonathan said, "Thank you for inviting me to dinner."

"I'm looking forward to it." Vlad flashed his toothy smile. "Do you like steak?"

"Sure, but don't go to any trouble."

"It's my favorite food." Vlad winked at him. "I like it rare."

As Jonathan opened the door, the two dogs stood on either side of their masters, forcing the two men closer together. Jonathan's knees buckled underneath him. Looking up at Vlad's perfectly proportioned features, Jonathan heard himself say, "By the way, I've always suspected Dracula was gay, and that he and Jonathan Harker were lovers."

Vlad rested his long fingers on Jonathan's small shoulder. "Then that's another way Dracula and I are different. I'm straight. See you tonight."

Jonathan's jaw dropped as Vlad and Barnabas left for Bungalow Four.

* * *

As Cal exited Bungalow One, he waved to Vlad Lesti entering Bungalow Four with his dog. Since Carla had been too nauseous to get out of bed, Cal had brought her breakfast, amidst her declarations that she would have her womb sewn closed after she finally gave birth.

Cal went into the main bungalow, walked through the front porch and living room, and joined Michael at the kitchen table. He was eating the three-berry waffles topped with Greek yogurt Cal had made for him.

Cal fed Michael a strawberry. "How did Billy Dean do yesterday?"

"Fine. He's a good worker."

"And quite a character."

"Like I was when we met." Michael gave Cal a sweet smile.

"How did things go at Tommy's last night?" Cal asked.

Michael swallowed his juice. "They went."

"That exciting, huh?"

"I was busy serving everybody their drinks, but I couldn't stop thinking about Malcolm."

"Malcolm?"

"In Bungalow Two. After I brought his bag inside, he asked to see one of my articles."

"That's terrific! When are you going to bring it to him?"

"This afternoon." Michael lowered his head.

"Something wrong with afternoons?"

"My only published piece is the one about young gays voting."

"Did Republicans make a law against young gays voting?"

Michael sighed. "Malcolm says we're a niche market."

"But a cute niche." Cal kissed Michael's velvety cheek.

"Malcolm's magazine is geared toward straight people."

"Like pretty much everything in news and entertainment. That's why we need 'niche' newspapers, magazines, websites, books, movies, and TV shows. For groups who don't feel represented by the mainstream."

Michael finished his breakfast. "I just hope Malcolm doesn't think I'm..."

"What? Gay? Young? Black?"

"No. Unable to shoot photos for the average reader."

"Michael, the 'not average' reader pays for magazines too. Besides, a good photojournalist is a good photojournalist. And what does Malcolm have against young gay guys? I assume he was once one himself."

"Malcolm's on the down-low."

Cal laughed out loud. He was not one to mock someone's decision whether or not to come out of the closet, but the whole down-low thing seemed incredibly hypocritical and destructive to him.

"So you think it's okay for gay guys like Malcolm to pretend to be straight, including to their families?"

Michael pushed his plate away. "I didn't say that."

"What are you saying, Michael?"

Michael rested his elbows on the table. "I want to be successful like Malcolm. And I think I can learn a lot from him."

"Fine. Divorce me, marry a woman, and tell everyone you're straight."

"That's not what I mean."

Cal rose, cleared the table, and loaded the dishwasher. "What do you mean, Michael?"

"Fortune landed Malcolm Wolf at my doorstep. I don't want to screw things up."

"You won't. Just be yourself. And show Malcolm your good work."

"Okay."

They met at the sink. Cal wrapped his arms around his husband. The hug was warm and comforting. "You want to make our son proud of his younger old man, don't you?"

Michael kissed Cal's nose. "Cal Cozzi V will be proud of his roots. Just like you are."

"I almost forgot. I found my great-grandfather's diary behind a loose piece of molding in our bedroom."

Michael did a double take. "It survived all this time?"

"Looks like it. After the long day yesterday, I read the first two entries before falling asleep. I'm looking forward to reading more tonight."

"That's great, Cal," Michael said with a melancholy smile, as if demonstrating cognitive dissonance for a psychology class.

"Don't look so excited."

"I am excited. For you, and for our son."

"Michael, our son will know about his Rodgers side too."

Michael laughed wistfully. "Right. How his father was dirt poor, escaped a homeless shelter when his parents died, and tried to mug his soon-to-be husband in an alley after his brother committed suicide."

Cal rubbed Michael's wide muscled back. "Is that what this roots thing is about? You're worried our son will revel in his Cozzi side and be embarrassed by his Rodgers side?"

"It's more than that." Michael pulled away to look into his eyes. "You have roots here in Cozzi Cove. I don't. It's your home. Not mine."

"It's your home too because you married me."

"Exactly."

"Do you want us to leave Cozzi Cove?"

"That's not what I want. And you wouldn't do it even if I asked."

Cal took Michael's hand and kissed it. "Michael, all new parents have some angst about whether or not they'll be good at it. After all the books we've read, the clips we've watched on the web, and the baby things we've bought to fill the back bedroom, I still toss and turn at night, panicked over whether or not we're doing the right thing." He rested Michael's head on his chest. "But then I think about how much I love you, and how much you love me. And I know our son will have everything he'll need."

They shared a long, wet kiss.

"How y'all doing this morning?" Billy Dean called out from the living room.

Cal and Michael walked to the front room to find Billy Dean waiting. Today, he was wearing a peach tank top and white shorts that showed off his bulging muscles.

"Good morning, Billy Dean. Ready for duty?"

Billy Dean saluted Cal. "As Grampa would say, 'I'm ready as a dog at a clumsy man's barbecue.'"

Cal smiled.

Michael asked, "Do you remember your duties?"

Billy Dean nodded. "I'll pick up my cart in the shed and start with Bungalow One."

"You might want to hold off a while on cleaning Bungalow One," Cal said.

"Unless you want an angry pregnant woman to hurl the cart at you," Michael said with a smile.

Billy Dean was nonplussed. "Okay, I'll start with Bungalow Two."

Michael added, "If Malcolm Wolf is there, please tell him I'll be over with my article this afternoon."

"Will do," Billy Dean replied as he went out the front door.

* * *

That afternoon, with his heart pounding in his ears, Michael knocked on the door of Bungalow Two, laptop in hand. Malcolm Wolf opened the door wearing a lime Speedo. Michael couldn't help noticing Malcolm's wide pectoral muscles and washboard abdominals.

"Michael, come in."

Michael followed Malcolm into the living room.

"I just returned from the main beach. What a beautiful day. I may never want to leave Cozzi again. Give me two minutes to stand under the shower, and then I want to read your work. Make yourself comfortable." Malcolm gestured to a pitcher and two glasses on the end table. "Help yourself to some lemonade."

A little while after Malcolm disappeared into the bathroom, the sound of water droplets pounding against the shower glass reached Michael, and he was reminded of his perspiration-soaked short-sleeved shirt. He paced the living room, staring out at the cove, hoping to get some solace from the calm bay water lapping against the white sand and mosaic rocks.

Malcolm startled Michael out of his meditation when he entered the room with a white towel tied around his waist and said, "Please, have a seat. I'll be right out." Malcolm disappeared into the front bedroom, leaving the door ajar.

From where he was standing, Michael couldn't help notice Malcolm drop the towel onto the bed, revealing a wide V-shaped back, round muscular buttocks, and sculpted thighs. He was glued to the spot. Michael gasped when Malcolm turned around, displaying the longest and thickest dick he'd ever seen.

Malcolm looked up and smiled at Michael as he slipped into his briefs, shorts, polo shirt, and sandals. He then entered the living room and sat on the sofa. "Please, join me."

Michael did as Malcolm asked, feeling like a serf granted a visit by a king.

"Let's see what you've brought me."

Michael opened the laptop, tapped a few keys, and then handed it to Malcolm, trying to still his shaking hand. He held his breath as Malcolm slowly examined the photographs in the article.

Malcolm looked up. "Hm."

"I know it's a niche article," Michael explained.

"That it is."

"And it's my first published piece."

"I understand."

"But the editor was happy with it."

"I can see why."

"You think it's okay?"

"No."

Michael's heart dropped to his stomach.

"I think it's great."

"You do?" Michael couldn't believe his ears.

"The photos are clear with good line, texture, colors, shading, and composition. They illustrate the story quite well with a nice beginning, middle, and end. They also help tell the who, what, where, when, and why of the piece. Each picture will show up perfectly in print and on the web." Malcolm turned to Michael. "Good job, young man."

Michael wanted to do a cartwheel, but he maintained his composure. "Thank you, sir."

"Please, it's Malcolm. You sure you don't want any lemonade?"

Michael's throat was so dry he could barely swallow. "Actually, I'd love some."

After they both finished their drinks, Michael slid forward on the sofa and took back his laptop. "Thank you so much for looking at my article."

"It was my pleasure." Malcolm smiled. "You're a good photographer and a fine storyteller."

Michael closed the laptop, shook Malcolm's hand, and then shook it again. "Thank you, Malcolm."

"Let's do this," Malcolm said, leaning back on the sofa. "Compose an article for me with photos about what men are wearing at the beach and why. Don't make it a gay thing. Shoot straight guys. And make sure there are more white guys than black guys in the pictures, so it doesn't come off like a racial piece."

Michael was thrilled for the opportunity to impress someone like Malcolm Wolf. "Should the shots be more news oriented or entertainment slanted?"

"There's no difference nowadays. And don't worry about authenticity. Nobody does fact-checking nowadays. Just take some provocative pictures in a sequence that draws in the audience. You've got forty-eight hours."

"What happens if you don't like it?"

"You spent forty-eight hours snapping pictures of men in bathing suits."

"And if you like it?"

"I'll compliment your good work." Malcolm pulled up Michael's chin with his thick thumb. "You didn't ask me what would happen if I love it?"

Michael perked up. "If you love the article?"

Malcolm laughed. "Let's cross that bridge when we come to it. Michael, I know, like most young people, you're looking for a job, and I'm happy you're interested in working for me. But it's a very competitive field. Lots of young people, and older ones, too, would give their firstborn to have an opportunity like I'm giving you."

"And I really appreciate it, Malcolm."

"Good. You should." Malcolm rested his large hand on Michael's knee. "So we'll take this one step at a time. Let me get a sense of your talents, and see if I think you're someone who would fit in at my magazine."

"I don't know what to say."

"Say you'll do a great piece for me. And you'll be open to my critique."

Michael knew a great deal about critique sessions from his college classes, where his professors and classmates had sometimes nearly brought him to tears. But he'd learned an enormous amount from those sessions, and he valued them as important tools for growth.

"I'm totally open to anything you might throw my way."

"Good." Malcolm squeezed Michael's knee. "It's too early to tell. But I think you and I might come to a mutually beneficial agreement."

"I'm really excited about the possibility, Malcolm."

Malcolm smiled at him. "Me too."

Michael left Malcolm's bungalow, nodded to Nijad Hadad as they passed each other, and continued along the cove toward the main bungalow feeling like a kid in a candy factory.

* * *

At one o'clock on the dot, Nijad Hadad, wearing a white polo shirt and chocolate-colored shorts, knocked on the door of Bungalow Six. A beautiful woman in a pink blouse and white shorts and sandals answered the door. Long blonde hair cascaded down the sides of her milky-white face. Crystal-blue eyes sparkled under long lashes and a button nose led to full ruby-red lips. His shorts grew tighter.

"Hello, I'm Nijad. Are you Annabel?"

"Yes?"

Nijad noticed the trace of a British accent. "It's a pleasure to meet you, Annabel."

"You too, Nijad." Annabel's soft hand melted inside Nijad's.

He didn't want to let go. "I have a date with Andrew."

"Right."

"Is he in?"

"No. Yes." She smiled. "Andrew was going to ring you up last night, but he didn't have your mobile number."

"Why?"

When Nijad finally released her hand, Annabel said, "My brother's feeling a bit poorly."

"I hope he's all right."

"He must have eaten something that didn't agree with him last night at the restaurant. He was stuck in the loo for most of the night, poor chap."

Nijad thought it must have been the lobster-stuffed sole since Nijad had slept quite well. "I'm sorry to hear that."

"Spending the day and night in bed should render him fit by tomorrow."

"Please tell him I hope he feels better, and that we can postpone our outing until he's up to it."

Annabel bit at a perfectly manicured pink nail. "Actually, I'm the one who adores miniature golf. Andrew detests it. Especially trying to get the ball under the blasted windmill."

They laughed together.

"He also hates me trying to take care of him."

Nijad scratched his dark hair. "What will you do all day?"

"I haven't the foggiest."

"Would you like to accompany me this afternoon?" Nijad was sorry not to have a date with Andrew, but he couldn't ignore his equal attraction to his twin sister. "If you think it's all right to leave Andrew alone, that is."

"I don't believe Andrew will have a problem with it."

"Then I'm game. No pun intended."

"Let me get my purse, and we'll be off."

Nijad drove Annabel to the miniature golf center in town. He parked, and they entered the large building. After paying the admission and selecting their golf clubs and balls, they headed to the winding course and proceeded to play, hitting their balls into a plastic clown's mouth, over a baby dinosaur's tail, through a tiny lake, into an elephant's trunk, and, finally, under the rotating mini windmill.

After Annabel had won three out of three games, they left the golf center, and Nijad bought them frozen vanilla custard. They sat on the park bench enjoying the cool, sweet, and creamy snack.

Annabel looked around the park at the kelly-green trees, multicolored flowers, babbling brook, and bronze statue of Cal Cozzi I. "What a lovely place."

"Agreed." Nijad smiled. "You're quite the miniature golf player."

"I played mini golf in Kent all the time. Other adults thought I was barmy."

"I've been to England but never to Kent. Did you enjoy living there?"

Annabel nodded. "The gardens, abbeys, and caves are smashing. And of course there's Canterbury Cathedral, the White Cliffs of Dover, and my favorite, Leeds Castle."

"Would you like to live in a mansion like that someday?"

"As a flight attendant, the joke is on me if I would, isn't it?" She laughed and ate her dessert.

"Do you like being a flight attendant?" Nijad asked.

"I like traveling, so I'd be silly to do anything else."

"Except be a pilot, a spy, or a travel agent." He winked at her.

"A travel agent, like you."

"How do you know?"

"Andrew told me. Do you like it?"

"Very much. It allows me to visit glorious places like Cozzi Cove, and meet fascinating people like you and Andrew. How's he feeling, by the way?"

"Andrew?"

"Yes. As his twin, can't you tell by just thinking about him?"

"There are times when I feel what Andrew is feeling, and I think just like him." She gave him a radiant grin. "He's feeling better, and he really likes you by the way."

Nijad's cheeks flushed. "We had an amazing dinner last night." He winced. "I'm sorry he got sick."

"Why didn't you two have a shag afterward?"

Nijad nearly fell off the bench. "It was our first date!"

"Ah, a gentleman. I wish I'd known men like you when I was in college."

"I wish I'd known *you* back in college. Do you have a boyfriend or husband?"

"Cheeky, aren't you?"

He blushed. "I apologize if I'm prying."

"Not at all."

"But you didn't answer my question."

They giggled.

Annabel replied, "I've gone out with quite a few guys, but I haven't been serious with any of them."

"Why is that?"

"Some were a bit dodgy. Others were nice, but things simply didn't work out when they got to know me."

Nijad smiled. "Secrets have you?"

"Doesn't everyone?"

"Your brother said he has secrets too."

"He does."

"It's good that you and Andrew are so close."

She nodded. "I'm sure Andrew told you our mother was quite wonky."

"He didn't give me the details."

"He no doubt wanted to spare you. Here's an illustration for you. I remember when my mum caught me putting on her makeup. I must have been about five years. She beat me with her wooden spoon until I bled. The more I cried, the harder she hit. She'd be joyous one minute and vicious the next. She was a very unhappy woman. Less happy the rare times my dad was home. If Andrew and I hadn't had each other for support, I don't think we'd have made it through. We no longer speak to Mum, which is fine with her, and with us."

Nijad took her hand in his. "I'm sorry that happened to you and Andrew."

"You're a nice man, Nijad." She looked at him and smiled. "I'm glad you met Andrew."

"I'm glad I met both of you at Cozzi Cove."

"Yes, Cozzi Cove is a wonderful place. Perfect for a week's holiday."

"I hope to spend more time with both of you if possible." Nijad moved closer to her on the bench. "I'm guessing Andrew told you I'm bisexual."

"Yes, he informed me through the bathroom door." She sat back, looking deep in thought.

"What are you thinking about?"

"How much I like you."

"Good. I like you too."

"And I was thinking how the three of us could be ripe for a daytime show on the telly."

Nijad laughed. "I hadn't thought of that. Do we have a dilemma?"

"I believe so."

"How about this?" Nijad tented his fingers. "Let's say we all spend the week together, no strings attached. And let's see what transpires."

"But Andrew saw you first."

"And I like Andrew a great deal. But I'd like to be friends with you too. All right?"

"All right."

They spent the next few hours strolling around the quaint town of Cozzi.

As Nijad drove back to Cozzi Cove, he marveled at how lucky he was to have met two people he liked on his vacation. He might have to pick one twin over the over, but hoped that time wouldn't come too soon.

At the entrance to Bungalow Six, Nijad pulled Annabel in for a good-bye kiss on the cheek, running his hand down her soft back. Annabel pulled away.

"I better check in on Andrew."

"Please give him my best. Can I see you both tomorrow?"

"How about lunch and a walk around town? Andrew and I can sit on opposite sides of you at the Cozzi Diner like two biscuits surrounding sweet cream."

"It sounds...sweet."

"Come to our bungalow at noon."

"I look forward to it. Please give Andrew my best."

"I will." Annabel waved and closed the door behind her.

Nijad nodded at the houseboy out on the cove, and returned to his bungalow feeling lighter than air.

* * *

Billy Dean Boyd had turned down all the beds and returned his maid's cart to the shed. He was heading toward his bicycle in the Cozzi Cove parking lot, but he stopped at the cove. He'd been so busy all day cleaning, restocking, and doing turndown service in the bungalows he hadn't taken any time to enjoy the beauty of Cozzi Cove.

Billy Dean sat on a large rock. He took in a deep salty breath and gazed out at the tranquil baby-blue sky adorned with swirls of creamy clouds hovering over the sun-kissed bay. Staring out at the old lighthouse in the distance, Billy Dean couldn't deny the fact that he was growing more and more horny each day, each hour, each minute. The other boys in his high school back home signed their virgin cards and then headed with their girlfriends to the haylofts, happier than a bull with two dicks. And in college, the guys on his football team were screwing like rabbits. A few of them had even made passes at Billy Dean. He couldn't count the guys and girls in his play who had made it crystal clear they wanted a lot of Li'l Abner. And Billy Dean was attracted to many of them. He'd wanted to neck out in the moonlight with Moonbeam McSwine, roll around in the hay with Hairless Joe, and quench his loneliness with Lonesome Polecat. General Bullmoose seemed to have a bull of a dick, and Evil-Eye Fleegle wasn't evil at all. But Billy Dean had made a promise to Jesus that he would remain chaste until marriage. And he loved Jesus with all his mind, heart, soul, and spirit. He couldn't let Jesus down.

Billy Dean's eyes closed. He wasn't quite sure how much time had gone by when he opened them to see Jesus standing on the white sand in front of him. Just as Billy Dean had imagined him, Jesus was tall and thin with long dark hair and a soft beard. He was handsome, with striking features; his skin was the color and texture of milk chocolate, his eyes dark and pensive. As when John the Baptist baptized him, Jesus stood in his white loincloth at the water's edge with the sun casting a golden halo over him. He beckoned to Billy Dean.

Billy Dean leapt from the rock and happily approached his savior. "Jesus?"

"Yes."

Billy Dean wondered why Jesus spoke English. Then he realized that as the son of God, Jesus would be able to speak any language he wanted to speak. "Thank you for visiting me."

Jesus's voice was warm and smooth like velvet tossed in a summer breeze. "It's my pleasure."

Up close, Billy Dean noticed the scars on Jesus's head and hands, no doubt from the crown of thorns and nails during his crucifixion. "I've longed to see you, Jesus."

"Thank you."

Another man of about thirty years old approached them wearing a white loincloth. While his hair, beard, and coloring matched Jesus's, his features were wider and more prominent.

"This is John," Jesus said to Billy Dean.

Tears came to Billy Dean's eyes. "John is your favorite. He rests on your chest, and you told your mother to call John 'her son.'"

"That's right," Jesus said.

"And you two love each other," Billy Dean added.

"Yes, we do," John said of his messiah.

"I love you too," Billy Dean said to Jesus. "I want to be with you." Billy Dean couldn't have been more thrilled to be in the presence of his biblical heroes and spiritual royalty.

Jesus and John smiled at each other, and then Jesus replied, "We want to be with you too."

Billy Dean was incredibly honored. He fell to his knees to praise and worship his lord.

Jesus touched Billy Dean's hand and pulled him to his feet. The warmth of Jesus's touch flew up his arm and cascaded through his entire body. Jesus slowly and softly cradled Billy Dean and rested Billy Dean's head on his chest, as Billy Dean reveled in the arms of his lord.

John walked behind Billy Dean and placed his hands on Billy Dean's back as if soft, warm rose petals had landed there.

Jesus raised Billy Dean's head to his and placed a gentle kiss on his lips. Billy Dean could barely feel it, but he knew it was a special gift from the son of God.

John gently turned Billy Dean to face him and did the same, like a kiss from an angel.

The three of them shared another kiss. Billy Dean's body was weightless, and his mind was foggy yet totally present. His spirit danced.

Jesus and John undressed Billy Dean, removing his T-shirt and shorts. Billy Dean wondered if he was going to get baptized in the bay when the two men then took off their loincloths. But Jesus reached for

Billy Dean, pulling him to his chest, and Billy Dean returned the hug. He rested his cheek against the soft black hair on Jesus's chest and touched the scars on his back where the Roman soldiers must have whipped him.

When Jesus lifted Billy Dean's face and pressed their lips together, Billy Dean's growing erection made him step back in embarrassment. But Jesus smiled and took him back in his arms as John stepped behind Billy Dean and massaged his back.

John brushed his lips against Billy Dean's neck and then leaned in to kiss Jesus. They broke apart and kissed Billy Dean. Jesus gently pushed Billy Dean back against John's chest and bent to kiss his neck and stroke his genitals.

Billy Dean pulled away and looked at Jesus. "Is this all right?"

Jesus nodded.

When Billy Dean looked back to John, he did the same.

Jesus and John kept Billy Dean sandwiched between them as the three kissed, cuddled, and caressed each other. He quickly exploded in orgasm as he rested his head on Jesus's shoulder and clasped his hands up and around the back of John's neck, keeping him close. They all kissed again.

Then Jesus and John headed into the bay as if it were the Sea of Galilee. Jesus looked back and beckoned Billy Dean to follow them. The three men swam and treaded water, and then Billy Dean followed Jesus and John back to the shore. Jesus and John lay on the white sand to dry their bodies under the sun. They motioned for Billy Dean to lie between them. Billy Dean complied and rested his head on Jesus's chest, held John's hand, and peacefully closed his eyes.

When Billy Dean opened his eyes some time later, he was lying alone on the white sand.

CHAPTER FOUR

That evening in Bungalow Three, Jonathan Harper tried on three dress shirts before he settled on the purple one with the gray slacks. He had spent his day at the Horror Convention watching Vlad Lesti play Dracula in a roped-off area and barely noticing anything happening at the booths. Vlad seemed to relish his role as seducer, phantom of darkness, and vampire legend. He twirled his cape, exposed his fangs, and beckoned attendees to join him for a simulated bite on the neck. The guests giggled and gawked in delight as his fake fangs, previously dipped in red dye, grazed their necks. When they left the "stage" area, Vlad gave each guest a pint of "blood"—a tomato juice concoction. Jonathan so longed to be one of Vlad's patrons, but he remembered the actor's request not to cause him to break character. Besides, by some twist of fate, Jonathan had his own private dinner date with Count Dracula that evening, or rather with Vlad Lesti—who said he was straight.

When Jonathan was tired of changing shirts, he left his bungalow with gift in hand and Renfield at his side, and knocked on the door of Bungalow Four. Vlad answered quickly, looking amazing with his long dark hair hanging down to just above his broad shoulders. He wore black slacks and a white ruffled shirt that showed off a lean, firm chest.

"Jonathan. Renfield. Welcome."

Renfield stood still, gazing at Vlad. Jonathan handed Vlad the bottle of wine.

Vlad took it gratefully. "My favorite. Red. Please, come in." He led Jonathan and Renfield through the front porch into the living room.

Jonathan couldn't help taking a peek into the front bedroom.

Vlad smiled. "If you're looking for my coffin. I keep it in the rear bedroom."

As they passed the rear bedroom, Jonathan noticed the door was closed. Moving through the kitchen, Jonathan and Renfield followed Vlad out the back door to the coral stone patio.

Once Renfield and Barnabas were happily licking, sniffing, and cuddling under the white oak table, Jonathan and Vlad sat across from each other on the white wicker chairs.

Vlad said, "It's amazing how well our dogs get along."

"It will be sad for them to separate next week," Jonathan replied.

"Where do you live?" Vlad opened the wine and poured.

"In Trenton."

"What do you do?"

"I'm a tax auditor."

"Ah. I live in New York City. Not too far away. Maybe we can schedule a doggy visit." Vlad winked at him. "And a doggy daddy visit too, except no tax audit. I'm an actor. I don't make enough money to be audited."

"I've audited some actors."

"But I bet I'm more fun."

Jonathan's social life revolved around watching gay porn on the web. He couldn't understand why a straight man was flirting with him. *Gay men never flirted with him.* And generally, straight men treated Jonathan like an alien from outer space since he had no interest in sports, cars, rock music, or dating women.

"You shared with me this morning that you're straight."

"That's right. I'm guessing you're gay."

"Good guess."

"Are you going to say I can read minds like Dracula?"

"No, I'm going to ask why you're staying at a gay resort."

Vlad looked up at the stars twinkling in the Persian blue sky. "Cozzi Cove is a gorgeous place. And it's close to the convention. Is it a problem that I'm staying here?"

"Not for me." Jonathan looked down at Renfield. "And clearly not for Renfield either."

"Good." Vlad raised his wine glass. "To new friends, and questionable lineage." After they toasted, he took a long sip of wine. "Delicious."

Jonathan nursed his. "I agree that Cozzi Cove is an amazing place, but doesn't it make you feel self-conscious to be around so many gay men?"

"I'm an actor. I'd never work if I were homophobic."

Jonathan was reminded of Vlad's performance at the convention. "You did a great job today. I wasn't the only one who believed you were Dracula."

"Thanks." Vlad smiled. "It beats sitting in an office all day. No offense."

"None taken. Mostly, I visit people who don't want to meet with me."

"Sounds ghastly."

"I enjoy it."

Vlad rubbed his chiseled chin. "I've never played a tax auditor."

"What other acting jobs have you done, besides playing the sponge and the pickle?"

Vlad laughed. "Yes, my theatrical triumphs." He rested back in his chair. "You'll like this. I played a bat in a touring play for children, and Dorian Gray in an off-Broadway play."

"Dracula, like Dorian Gray, never grew older."

"Are you still convinced I have some connection with Dracula?"

"Did you compile a list of the names and locations of all your relatives who are older than you?"

Vlad dug into his pocket and handed Jonathan a piece of paper. "That's the best I could do."

Jonathan scanned it, then put it in his pocket. "I'll run it through the web program and see what comes up."

Vlad finished his wine. "Why is it so important to you?"

"I told you. I have a sixth sense about these things."

"I meant the Horror Convention. Why do you go to them?"

"They're entertaining, enlightening, and full of the world of make-believe."

"Why is that so vital for you?"

"I was a small, thin, weak, gay kid. That meant I was picked on a lot. Amidst the name calling, pushing, and pranks, the portal out of my misery was fantasy."

"Why vampires specifically?"

Jonathan's cheeks burned. "I always found them sexy. And I'm fascinated by the historical connections of the undead."

"The undead?"

"Witches, warlocks, ghosts, vampires, werewolves. Their legends, origins, stories, characters. But what entices me the most is the possibility of hope."

"Hope?"

Jonathan nodded. "That the world as we know it isn't the only reality. What if there's another plain of existence where everyone is welcome, other power sources exist, nobody ever dies, and darkness comes into the light?"

Vlad smiled. "You're an interesting guy."

"Nobody's ever told me that before."

"Then they never took the time to get to know you." Vlad gazed at Jonathan across the candlelight. "Thank you for joining me for dinner."

"My pleasure."

Vlad lifted the warming covers from their plates and steak dinners emerged. Vlad's was swimming in blood.

Jonathan laughed. "I think our dogs would send that back for more time in the oven."

"Which reminds me." Vlad served the grateful dogs their steak dinners under the table.

Jonathan admired his own medium steak, baked potato with sour cream and chives, and peas and carrots.

"I eat simply," Vlad said. "I'm allergic to a number of spices, like parsley and garlic."

Jonathan raised an eyebrow. "You're allergic to garlic?"

Vlad laughed. "I know what you're thinking. People do have food allergies."

"Of course." Jonathan dug into the delicious dinner. "You're a very good cook."

"Living alone for so many years, I had to learn to cook or starve."

"You've never been married?"

Vlad speared a piece of bloody meat. "I've come close a few times, but it never happened."

"How come, if you don't mind me asking?"

"I don't mind at all. One girlfriend wanted a stable provider, and the actor's life wasn't for her. Another just didn't get me. The latest one had no sense of humor."

"Were they all women?"

Vlad narrowed his eyes. "Are you one of those gay guys who thinks every man is gay?"

"Not really." Jonathan looked away, realizing he was exactly that kind of gay guy.

"How about this? You can continue thinking I'm a descendant of a vampire, but you have to accept that I'm straight. Deal?"

Jonathan shrugged. "Sure."

They enjoyed their dinners. Then Renfield and Barnabas, having finished theirs, chased each other, running around them in a circle. Vlad said, "Looks like our dogs need some exercise. Care for a stroll on the cove?"

"I'd like that."

As they walked on the white sand, listening to the Duke-blue waves lap against the carved rocks, Vlad gazed out at the gray lighthouse in the distance. "What a magnificent place."

"Have you traveled a great deal?" Jonathan asked.

"Mostly in the US, doing shows."

"I'm surprised."

"Why?"

"You have a European way about you."

"That's because I'm a vampire, or rather, playing one this week."

"Do you find yourself taking on the roles you play?"

"As an actor, I connect with all my roles. It's part of my job to accurately and realistically portray a character by getting into his head and heart."

"Did you do some research on Dracula?"

"Sure. I read the book, saw the movies and TV shows."

"Don't actors use sense memory and emotional recall, where you remember past experiences from your own life to connect with the character you are portraying?"

"You're relentless. No, I've never bitten anyone." He giggled. "At least I've never drawn blood." Vlad stopped at the sound of a sudden yelp.

Renfield and Barnabas had been playing in the sand, but it appeared Renfield's paw was now caught under a boulder. Vlad rushed over to the dog, lifted the boulder into the air, and Renfield was free. After replacing the boulder, Vlad knelt down, inspected Renfield's paw, and made eye contact with him. And with that, the dog stopped yelping. A moment later, Renfield hurried off to play with Barnabas.

"How did you do that?" Jonathan asked.

"Do what?"

"Lift that boulder and calm Renfield down?"

"I told you. I lift weights at the gym, and I'm a dog lover." Vlad looked at Jonathan and shook his head. "You ask a lot of questions." He went to sit on a nearby rock.

Jonathan followed to sit on a rock next to Vlad's. "It's probably a rollover from my job."

"Never mind. I'd rather you ask me about being a vampire than about my taxes," Vlad said, grinning at Jonathan.

"How do your parents feel about you being an actor?" Jonathan asked, smiling back at him.

"They're thankful my brother is a doctor and my sister is an accountant," Vlad said with a chuckle. "They've given up on me. But they were proud when I was on the soap."

"Who did you play?"

"Unfortunately, a villain. So I didn't last too long." Vlad picked up a pebble and threw it into the bay. "We've been talking about me for most of the night. Not altogether a bad thing for an actor. But before we say good night, I'd like you to tell me about Jonathan Harper."

This stopped Jonathan for a moment. Nobody had ever asked him to talk about himself. Recovering, he replied, "Let's see. My parents are deceased. I'm an only child. I don't do well on dates, which is fine since I rarely have any. My passion is the occult world. When I die I want to be buried in a mausoleum."

"Because of the vampire thing?"

"No, because I'm claustrophobic."

Vlad laughed wildly. "You're a really fun guy to hang out with. Do you want to get together for dinner again tomorrow night?"

Jonathan wished a good-looking gay man would be as charmed by him. "Sure. Come to my bungalow at seven. I'll have the results of the web analysis by then."

"I look forward to it." Vlad rose and offered his hand for Jonathan to take.

Jonathan put his small hand in Vlad's larger one and stood. As he gazed into them, Vlad's eyes, warm and strong, seemed to hypnotize him, and he didn't want to let go. They stood that way for quite a while with Vlad smiling at him.

Then Vlad said, "Good night, Jonathan."

"Good night, Vlad."

Vlad bent down to pet Renfield. "Good night, Renfield."

Renfield offered his paw, and Vlad shook it. Then he and Barnabas disappeared into Bungalow Four.

Jonathan sat on the rock at the cove with Renfield resting on the sand below him. Watching the sunset, he vowed that tomorrow was the day to find out the truth about Vlad Lesti.

* * *

Cal Cozzi sat on the front porch of the main bungalow staring out at the cove. Ribbons of scarlet, peach, and marigold wove through the sky, reflecting on the calm bay water. As the sky joined the water in turning indigo, Cal spotted Carla and Cal's sister, Taylor, approaching the front door.

"Look who graced our humble existence with her presence," Carla said to Cal as they entered the porch.

Cal stood and kissed Taylor's cheek. "Hi, sis. How many minutes can you stay before leaving for Egypt to meet with a prince about an oil deal that would destroy our environment?"

Carla added, "And make the rich get richer and the poor poorer?"

Cal's sister, two years older than him but sporting the same auburn hair and broad shoulders, narrowed her eyes into green slits. "You liberals claim to care about the masses, but look how you treat your own sister and wife, even after my heart attack. Have you no sympathy for the overworked?"

"But definitely not the underpaid," Carla said.

"And you two will get every penny of it when I die from exhaustion." Taylor plopped herself down on the glider. "Push me on this thing like you did when we were kids, Cal. On second thought, don't. You used to push me so hard I vomited."

"On my head," Cal added.

"Served you right." Taylor propped her feet up on the arm of the glider. "My ankles are swollen, and my breasts are sore."

Carla groaned. "That's because I told you on the phone about my pregnancy symptoms." She took a seat on the rocking chair.

"Are you saying I suffer from hysterical pregnancy?" Taylor asked with a flip of her long hair.

"I'm saying you suffer from 'everything is about Taylor' syndrome. You always have, and unfortunately for me, you always will."

Taylor waved a manicured hand at her wife. "Well, everything *should* be about me. It's only fair."

"Care to explain that one?" Cal asked as he sat on the other rocking chair.

Taylor spoke like a kindergarten teacher demonstrating how to tie a shoelace. "I work day and night to keep all of you in the lap of luxury."

Carla chuckled. "This from the woman with the apartments in Paris, Rome, Palm Beach, and Wall Street."

"All of which I need in order to meet with clients so I can invest their money to make more money." Taylor fanned herself. "I thought you finally put air conditioning into this place, Cal."

"I did," Cal replied.

"It must be another hot flash," Taylor said, feeling her forehead.

Carla rubbed her stomach. "Let me know when the baby starts kicking inside your stomach."

Taylor pointed a finger at her wife. "It was *your* decision to carry this kid."

"This *kid*?" Carla glared at her. "You mean your nephew?"

Taylor replied, "Don't blame me for not liking kids. It's Cal's fault."

"How is it *my* fault?" Cal asked.

"Because when we were little, I put you in my doll stroller and you fell out. Mom punished me for a week. I was traumatized beyond words. Nobody could like kids after that." Taylor sat up. "What kind of innkeeper are you, Cal? Don't you offer your guests something to drink?"

"Cozzi Cove isn't a bed and breakfast, but for my loving sister, I'll be right back with the iced tea."

Cal headed through the living room into the kitchen. As he fetched the iced tea in the refrigerator and three glasses from the cupboard, he smiled. He was a kid again with Taylor and their shared history in the bungalow. Cal returned to the porch and served the drinks.

"I hope there's no caffeine or sugar in this," Taylor said.

"Thank you for being concerned about the baby and me," Carla replied.

"I'm not. Caffeine and sugar keep me up at night."

"You don't sleep anyway," Carla said.

Cal said, "It's decaf tea with honey."

"Nothing herbal, I hope!" Taylor said, as if herbal tea was toxic.

"Just regular old decaf tea," Cal replied.

"Thank God." Taylor downed her drink in one gulp. "I'll leave the herbs, incense, astrology, crystals, numerology, and cosmology to my wife."

"Carla did the baby's charts, and he's going to be 'kind, strong, fair, honest, and quite successful,'" Cal said, like a father bragging about his child's first tooth.

"Of course he is. He's a Cozzi," Taylor replied.

Remembering Michael's concern about feeling left out, Cal said, "He's also a Rodgers."

"Not to mention whatever his egg donor was." Taylor rested her head on the palm of her hand. "How exactly did that all work?"

"You sent us to the clinic in New York City, Taylor," Cal said.

"And I paid the steep bill."

"You said it was a wedding present," Cal replied.

"It was. And you gave Carla and me a mixing bowl. Just saying."

"It was a nice mixing bowl," Cal said.

When Cal looked to Carla for confirmation, Carla said, "Haven't you learned by now not to listen to her? I stopped listening in third grade."

Taylor guffawed. "You had your claws out for me all through school, and after. I was a happily married straight woman when you caught me in your clutches."

Carla looked at Taylor as if Taylor was from another planet. "I'll ask your three ex-husbands about that, and my mother who caught you and me making out when we were teenagers."

Taylor replied, "I understand that I'm the most interesting person in Cozzi, but does everything have to be about me? I was asking about my nephew the test-tube baby."

Carla rubbed her lower back. "If I could get off this chair, I'd slap her face."

"Why is everyone picking on *me*?" Taylor added, "My lower back is killing me, Cal. Can you get me a pillow?"

Cal went into his bedroom and brought out pillows for both women.

Carla explained to Taylor, "The secret donor went to the clinic, where they extracted some of her eggs—"

"Start at the beginning, where Cal and Michael masturbated into little white cups," Taylor interrupted. "Cal, did they have gay magazines at the clinic? I always wondered about that."

His face flushing, Cal replied, "Yes, they had magazines."

"Did you and Michael go into the little bathroom together or one at a time?" Taylor asked.

Cal cleared his throat. "One at a time."

"Why?" Taylor insisted. "Can't you and Michael bring each other to orgasm? Maybe the clinic has a therapy for that." She considered. "But please don't use a sexual surrogate. Remember how conservative I am."

"Michael and I are fine," Cal answered.

Carla saved Cal from further embarrassment. "The clinic has certain procedures that everyone is asked to follow, including procedures for sperm collection."

Cal sat down on the rocking chair, hoping they'd change the subject.

Taylor arranged the pillow behind her back. "Since both you and Michael graced a cup with your manhood, how do we know which little seed matched with the egg donor's egg to hit Carla the Incubator and make my nephew?"

"If two sperm cells had fertilized two eggs, heaven forbid there could have been twins. Or the two fertilized eggs could have fused together to create one embryo," Carla explained.

"What if only one sperm hit a home run, and the other struck out with egg all over its face?" Taylor asked.

"Then only one us will be the biological father," Cal said.

"And that's okay with you?" Taylor asked her brother.

"Yes."

"I'll know by looking at him," Taylor said.

"You'll know what by looking at whom?" Carla asked her wife.

"The baby. Whether or not he's a Cozzi."

A crease formed between Cal's eyebrows. "Why is that so important?"

"Because we need an heir to this place," Taylor replied.

Cal did a double take. "You're always asking me to sell Cozzi Cove or turn it into condos. Now you want an heir for the next generation?"

"Of course." Taylor sat forward on the glider. "It's because I'm selfless, Cal. It's always been my major flaw. I know you want Cozzi Cove to continue being passed down to each generation of Cozzis. So, that's what I want for you. Though, personally, I think you should sell this place since even after the renovations it's still a bit in the red."

Cal sat next to her on the glider. "Our baby's biological father, and Cozzi Cove being in the red are the least of my worries right now, Taylor."

"What are you worried about, Cal?" Carla asked.

"Come with me."

Carla pried herself out of the rocking chair, and Taylor rubbed her own stomach as they followed Cal into the front bedroom.

"See that bookcase? It's full of every book ever written about taking care of a baby," Cal said.

"I'm impressed," Taylor said. "Do they have books on how to be nice to your sister who has devoted her life to you?"

Carla raised her eyes to the ceiling. "Ignore her, Cal."

"Step this way. And we're walking." Cal led them to the rear bedroom.

Taylor gasped at the contents of the room—wallpaper, rocking chair, bureau, crib, stroller, play station, safety seat, changing table, and washtub—all featuring cute zoo animals in adorable poses.

Cal opened the bureau drawers. "Undies, sleepwear, bibs, rattles, and thermometer," he said, holding up each item as if he were a spokesmodel on a television game show. He proceeded to the closet, opened it, and continued, "Blankets, breast pump, bottles, soap, shampoo, diapers, wipes, lotions, mobiles, night lights, and toys."

"Now I'm really impressed," Taylor said.

"And I'm getting shooting pains down my legs," Carla said.

"So am I!" Taylor added.

"Let's go back to the porch," Cal said.

Once they were seated again, with Taylor next to him on the glider, Cal said, "As you can see, Michael and I have been working very hard to make everything just right for the arrival of our baby."

Carla sighed and pushed herself slowly in the rocker. "Which I hope will be very soon."

"But?" Taylor asked Cal.

"There's still this nagging feeling in me that we aren't ready," Cal said.

"I'm definitely ready," Carla said.

"Cal," Taylor said, taking her brother's hands, "nobody will be a better father than you, even our own father, who was pretty terrific—except when I took the blame for you crashing his car."

Cal rubbed his temples. "We were playing together in Dad's car and you knocked into the emergency brake, causing the car to roll into a tree. When Dad came outside in a rage, you told him it was *my* fault."

"Then I pleaded your case to him, didn't I?"

"The world according to Taylor," Carla said.

Taylor sat back on the glider. "Speaking of which, I got a job offer."

"Why didn't you tell me?" Carla asked.

"I just did." Taylor's face lit up. "One of my clients offered me a CFO position at his company."

"What does he do?" Carla asked.

"He sells things."

"What?"

"Does it matter?"

Carla chuckled. "You're considering becoming the chief financial officer of a company, and you don't know what they sell? He could be in white slavery."

"There's not enough money in that. I checked into it a while ago for a client."

Carla threw up her hands.

"I'm his financial advisor. It doesn't matter to me what he sells, as long as it makes money," Taylor said as if it was the most obvious thing in the world.

"Are you going to take the job?" Cal asked.

"I'm tempted," Taylor replied. 'Traveling so much has taken a huge toll on me, as has running my own business."

"We hadn't noticed," Carla said with a knowing look to Cal.

"I know." Taylor sighed. "I don't complain about it, because I don't want to burden the people I support."

Cal and Carla shared a smirk.

"The salary and benefits are terrific," Taylor said.

"Is there anything higher than the top one percent?" Cal asked.

"This job may be it," Taylor said. "And I'd get to stay in one place and work shorter hours."

"It sounds ideal, sis. What's holding you back from accepting?"

"There's one tiny issue," Taylor said. "I'd have to live in Paris for most of the year."

Carla's hands shook as she lifted herself off the chair. "I'll say this only once, Taylor. Cozzi is our home. We were born here, met here, went to school here, fell in love here, and married here. Our families are here. Our lives are here. And this is where we will live, and die. Some of us sooner than others."

Taylor replied, "Don't be shy, Carla. Tell me what you really think."

"I think you aren't taking that job," Carla said.

"Just because we're married"—Taylor rose—"you can't make business decisions for me."

"I can, and I just have!"

Cal was getting whiplash from watching each woman make her declaration. "It sounds like you both need to talk about this, sleep on it, and then come to a joint decision."

Carla glared at her wife. "We'll talk about this all right."

Michael entered from the front door. Noticing the tension in the air, he asked, "Should I go back to Tommy's?"

Taylor sat back down on the glider and massaged her stomach. "I thought you got a college degree in something uselessly artsy, Michael. Why are you still working in that seedy bar?"

"It's not a seedy bar. It's Tommy's." Cal motioned for Michael to sit on his lap. "And Michael is talking with one of the guests at Cozzi Cove this week about a possible job working for his magazine."

When Michael told Taylor the name of the magazine, she was impressed. "Why would Malcolm Wolf want to hire *you*?"

"Thanks, sister-in-law," Michael said.

"That's the 'it' magazine right now. Wolf could get any photojournalist he wanted."

Cal defended his spouse. "Michael's great at what he does. Not many people can take top-notch photos that tell a story."

"Malcolm hasn't offered me a job yet. He wants to see my work," Michael explained.

"Are you sure that's all he wants to see?" Taylor asked with a grin.

Thinking about Malcolm Wolf living on the down-low, Cal hoped his sister was wrong. "Malcolm worked at Cozzi Cove during his first two years of college. Dad called him 'Mac.'"

"How old is he?" Taylor asked.

"Your age. But he didn't go to our high school. He lived in a neighboring town."

Taylor looked off into space. "I remember him." She smiled like the Cheshire cat. "He had a huge crush on you, Cal."

"If he did, I didn't know about it."

"You didn't know much about anything in those days, which is why I spent my entire childhood protecting you to my own detriment."

Cal blew a kiss to his sister.

Taylor said, "I hope Mac knows you're married, Cal." She gasped. "Wait a minute, I bet he planned this whole thing."

"What whole thing?" Cal asked.

Taylor turned to Carla. "You see how people with no business sense are totally naïve?"

Carla replied, "I own and manage a restaurant and I don't have the faintest idea what the hell you're talking about, Taylor. Please explain fast before my water breaks and leaks into the bay and none of us notice because as usual we're all focused on your delusions."

"It may not be a delusion." Taylor slid to the edge of the glider and spoke like a school librarian reading a story to captivated children. "Eighteen-year-old Malcolm Wolf was madly infatuated with sixteen year-old Cal Cozzi who didn't return Malcolm's affections. Seventeen years later, Malcolm comes back to Cozzi Cove, a rich, successful businessman. He seduces Cal's young husband with a job offer that turns into seduction of a different kind. The young husband takes the bait, pardon the pun, and leaves Cal Cozzi for a life of journalistic excitement with Malcolm Wolf. One week later, Malcolm dumps said young husband. Too embarrassed to return back to his older and wiser husband, the young runaway spends the rest of his life destitute, in poverty, shame, loneliness, and remorse. Malcolm Wolf revels in his revenge!" Taylor bowed.

Carla groaned. "That's the stupidest story I've ever heard."

"And totally unfounded." Cal explained, "Mac never made a pass at me back then."

"And he's been totally businesslike with me now," Michael said. "Besides, he's married to a woman, and he has two kids."

Taylor gasped. "Living on the down-low! Those guys are the most sexually aggressive. I should know."

"How should *you* know?" Carla asked.

Taylor replied, "Carla, while you stir your marinara sauce in the kitchen of your parents' restaurant, and putter around the tiny rooms above it, I live in the real world. As a beautiful, alluring woman who does business with all types of men, I have been propositioned numerous times by men on the down-low seeking a beard."

"How do you handle it?" Michael asked.

"I make investments for a mail-order bride company and for a male escort service. I share both phone numbers with the closet cases, and everyone's happy." Taylor wagged her finger at Michael. "I'm telling you, young, naïve, brother-in-law, be careful of Malcolm Wolf, or you'll end up back in that creepy alley where Cal picked you up."

"I can take care of myself." Michael folded his arms at his chest.

Taylor sat back on the glider. "Both of you, don't come crying to me when I'm right."

Michael asked, "When have I ever come crying to you, Taylor?"

"Maybe if you had, you wouldn't be pouring cheap beer for the local riffraff," Taylor replied.

"Stop picking on my husband." Cal put his arm around Michael and squeezed him into his chest. "He's been feeling down lately."

"Still?" Carla cocked her head in Michael's direction. "What's wrong, baby?"

"It's no big deal," Michael answered.

"Yes it is," Cal said.

"Sometimes I feel like I don't belong at Cozzi Cove."

"You don't." Taylor focused on the three gaping mouths. "What? Michael is a Cozzi by marriage only. Like Carla."

Carla rubbed her stomach. "You're lucky I love you so much, Taylor."

Michael said to Taylor, "Carla has roots here. So do you and Cal."

"Michael, your family has been in Cozzi as far back as you can remember," said Cal.

He laughed sardonically. "Yeah, living in run-down apartments."

"Cozzi Cove is your home, Michael," Cal said, meaning it.

"Until we turn it into condos," Taylor added.

"I'm sure glad I didn't listen to you on that one, sis." Remembering the diary, Cal said, "I found our great-grandfather's diary hidden behind a piece of molding in the front bedroom."

"What were you doing peering behind molding?" Taylor asked.

"I dropped a book on it. And to my surprise, I found the diary," Cal said.

Taylor seemed impressed. "It might be worth some money."

"Not to mention its emotional and familial worth." Carla turned to Cal. "If my wife had any sense, she'd have said that."

"I have plenty of sense," Taylor retorted. "That's why I've never kept a diary. A hundred years from now, I don't want some Cozzi reading all about my private thoughts."

"I don't blame you. They're pretty frightening." Carla winked at Cal.

Taylor asked Cal, "What does our great-grandfather have to say for himself?"

Cal slid to the edge of his seat, and Michael nearly fell off his lap. "I've only read the first two entries. But it's really interesting so far. Calvin I lost his father to tuberculosis and lost his wife in childbirth. He lived with his mother and baby boy."

"Our grandfather," Taylor inserted.

"Somehow I figured that out," Carla said.

Cal continued, "Great-granddad worked in a steel mill like his father, but they went on strike. Since he wrote the diary at thirty years old in 1937, and the New Deal was still two years away, he got the idea to build bungalows on the strip of land his father won in a card game at Tommy Malone's bar."

"Cozzi Cove, the family money pit." Taylor added, "Well, we know the end of the story. And with all of my aches and pains, I should get to bed." She rose.

"Are you staying over, sis?"

"Yes, I don't need to leave until the morning."

"Where are you going in the morning?" Cal asked, rising with Michael.

"Paris. But I'll be back."

"You better believe you will be." Carla struggled to get up.

"You ladies know your way home?" Cal asked with smirk.

"I think we'll manage," Carla said as they walked to the front door.

Taylor paused at the doorway and said, "Michael, get over yourself about your roots. You're a part of this family, whether you like it or not."

"Thanks, sister-in-law from hell." Michael kissed Taylor's cheek.

Taylor said to Carla as they left, "You see how they treat me? Me, who works my fingers to the bone, so they can live on the beach like surf bums."

Cal took the glasses to the kitchen and put them into the dishwasher. In the bedroom, he found Michael lying on their bed in his boxers.

Throwing off his own clothes, Cal joined his husband. "How was Tommy's?"

"Same old." Michael placed his laptop on his knees.

"What are you doing?"

"Starting my article."

"Your article?"

Michael nodded. "Malcolm gave me an assignment."

Cal hugged Michael to his chest. "You got a job!"

"Not exactly." He kissed Cal's chin. "It's kind of a test."

Cal peered over Michael's smooth shoulder. "What's the article about?"

"What men wear on the beach and why. I took some shots of a few guys at the main beach today and also at Tommy's. I need to edit and arrange them with captions."

"What did you find out?"

"Straight guys prefer long loose trunks." He tapped on his laptop.

"How about gay guys?"

"I don't know. I didn't ask any to pose for me."

"Why not?"

"Malcolm told me to concentrate on straight guys."

"That's a switch for you."

Michael pushed Cal away playfully. "I'm not the one who had sex with other guys before we met."

"And you won't have sex with any after, if I have anything to say about it." Cal nibbled on Michael's ear.

"Stop! I have work to do."

"Play first."

Cal kissed Michael's thick neck, a favorite spot for Michael. Then he slid the tip of his tongue around and inside Michael's ear. Michael gasped in delight.

After placing the laptop on Michael's night table, Cal slipped off Michael's boxers and then his own, and lay on top of him. Where their skin touched was like sizzling flames. Cal ran his hands through Michael's chestnut curls and enjoyed his vanilla scent. Then he kissed Michael deeply and tenderly, longing for the man he loved. Michael massaged Cal's rippling back and slid his hands down to squeeze his buttocks. Cal wanted to envelop Michael forever, place him in his heart, and never let him go.

They rolled over with Michael taking the dominant position. Cal let Michael have his fun, sucking and nibbling on Cal's pectorals, but Cal quickly turned the tables back to how he liked it. As he kissed and caressed Michael's soft skin, Cal lifted Michael's knees and slid inside him. Michael reacted with an appreciative moan that always sent Cal reeling. As they kissed, they built up a steady rhythm.

Michael whispered into Cal's ear, "You're my heart and my soul."

Cal whispered back, "Forever."

Cal couldn't hold back any longer. As the moon's glow bathed them in its special light, Cal rubbed Michael's thick shaft and head until they both let out a scream of joyous release. After, they lay in each other's arms, kissing and cuddling.

Cal said, "Cozzi Cove is your home, because I'm here."

"I'll always be by your side."

In minutes, Michael was snoring softly on Cal's chest. Unable to sleep, Cal gently lifted Michael's head and placed it onto his pillow. Then he turned on the pin light at his night table, grasped the diary, and opened to the third entry, the spot where he'd left off.

June 6, 1937.

A nineteen-year-old Negro man answered my ad in the newspaper for an assistant to help me build the bungalows at Cozzi Cove. He was well groomed with clean clothes and a friendly manner. He is smaller than me but stocky and strong. That's a good thing in house building. While Mama watched Calvin Jr. in the kitchen, I took the young man into the sitting room. His father is unemployed due to the auto strike. His mama is a maid for a wealthy family a few towns a way. She takes the bus to get there every morning and comes home late at night. The young man and I sat across from each other next to the fireplace. I could not believe how much we had in common. Like me, he enjoys reading books and building things. We like the same kind of architecture. We are both Democrats and Methodists, and we both swing to the music of Benny Goodman, Count Basie, and Duke Ellington. I could not believe it when I looked at my father's pocket watch and found two hours had gone by. I offered him the job on the spot. He agreed and left to pack his bag and move into our attic.

Tomorrow, we will start laying the foundations for the bungalows at Cozzi Cove. Oh, there is one other thing. He has these amazing dark, exotic eyes. He smells like sweet vanilla, and his smile makes me melt like butter. I had to hold myself back from taking him in my arms. That is my secret.

Cal rested his head on his pillow. As he drifted off to sleep, he thought about how he and his great-grandfather had a good many things in common.

CHAPTER FIVE

Cal woke early the next morning, showered, made goat cheese and asparagus omelets, and served them to Michael and Carla at the kitchen table.

"Did her majesty leave for Paris?" Cal asked Carla as he joined them at the table.

Carla nodded. "At six a.m. The little guy had been kicking me all night like a kung fu master. I had just fallen asleep when Taylor kissed me good-bye. I've been up ever since." She took a bite of her omelet. "How did you know I've been craving goat cheese?"

"You told me three times this week." Cal drank his juice. "George called. He and Aaron want you to surrogate a baby for them too."

Carla screamed. "Tell your brother I'm closed for renovations!"

"Did you do your breathing exercises this morning?" Cal asked.

"I breathed so much I hyperventilated," Carla replied.

"Did you say your positive affirmations into the mirror?" Michael asked.

Carla nodded. "If the 'universe lovingly supports me,' how come I feel as if my stomach is dragging on the ground?"

"Are you sure you want to use the midwife rather than go to the hospital?" Michael asked.

"You sound like Taylor. I'll tell you what I told her. I want my nephew to be brought into this world in a natural, safe, loving environment with positive energy. There's no place better for that than Cozzi Cove. If I change my mind when the time comes, knock me out and wake me up when Cal V is twenty-one."

Finished with his omelet, Michael said, "Did you and Taylor talk about her job offer last night?"

Carla sighed into her juice. "We had a few words. About a thousand of them." She added, "If we were starring in a network television show, the censors would have banned us."

Cal asked Carla, "So what's the verdict?"

"Taylor and I both have some thinking to do."

"I'd miss you both like crazy, but it would be nice for Taylor to stop all the traveling."

"Taylor can stop traveling and live in Cozzi Cove with me," Carla said.

"I can't imagine Taylor living in the apartment over your restaurant." Michael handed Carla her glass of milk. "Actually, I can't imagine Taylor living anywhere, except maybe in a palace."

"Taylor lived in this house for many years," Cal said.

"And it's time she returned to Cozzi." Carla drank some milk. After gagging, she asked Michael, "Any word from the magazine editor?"

"I have to work on a demo article for him today."

Carla buttered a piece of eight-grain toast, held it to her lips, and then tossed it onto her plate.

"Don't you like my toast?" Cal asked.

"I love it. It's the demon child who seems to hate everything I like." Carla focused on Cal. "Have you read any more of your great-grandfather's diary?"

Cal nodded. "I read another entry last night. It turns out great-grandpop had a lot more in common with me than his love for Cozzi Cove."

"Do tell." Carla slid to the edge of her seat and then rested her hands on the table to steady herself.

"It seems that Cal I had feelings for his assistant carpenter, a young local man," Cal said.

"Were the feelings returned by the young stud?" Carla asked.

Cal shrugged. "I haven't gotten that far."

Carla replied, "Read faster! Inquiring minds want to know."

When Carla went back to her bungalow and Michael was busy working on his article in the front bedroom, Cal headed out to the cove to water the plants. He was glad to see Billy Dean with his cart, servicing the rooms. When the boy came out of Bungalow Two, Cal stopped him.

"How are things going, Billy Dean?"

"Just fine. Thank you kindly for asking." Billy Dean squinted from the sun's rays. "It's already hotter than a fart on a griddle. I'm only up to Bungalow Three, and I'm sweating like a whore in church."

Cal smiled, realizing how important Billy Dean's grandfather was to the boy. "Feel free to take a break, Billy Dean."

"No need. There's nothing wrong with hard work. My grampa always said to me: 'You never get anywhere without hard work. Now go to work while I check the lottery number.'" Billy Dean smiled. "See you later, Cal."

Cal laughed as Billy Dean disappeared into Bungalow Three. With everything running well at Cozzi Cove, Cal headed back into the main bungalow front bedroom. He exchanged his T-shirt for a tank top and his long shorts for gym shorts. Then he kissed the top of Michael's head, left the bungalow, and drove into town. After parking out front, he entered the local gym for some stretching, followed by a half hour of cardio on the treadmill. Finally, Cal worked his shoulders and back at the lat pulldown machine.

"Enjoying your workout, Cal?" Malcolm Wolf sat up on a nearby bench. Having just bench-pressed twice his bodyweight, Malcolm looked like an Olympian with his muscles bulging out of a lemon-and-lime leotard top and black Lycra pants.

Cal took a break from his repetitions. "It helps clear the mind."

"Like being at Cozzi Cove. It's always been a magical place."

"I apologize for not recognizing you right away."

"It's understandable. I looked quite different. And I was the hired help. You were the gentry."

Cal frowned. "My father never thought of things that way, and neither did I. I still don't."

Malcolm rested his elbows on his large knees, causing his biceps to expand to the size of baseballs. "Your dad was a nice guy. He always treated me well."

"I agree."

"And you were pleasant and polite, always running off to football practice. I tried to pin you down to go to the movies with me once or twice. You wanted no part of it." Malcolm winked. "After meeting Michael, I realize your attractions are for light-skinned black men."

Cal's blood boiled. "I didn't fall in love with Michael for the color of his skin. And I didn't reject your offer to go to the movies when I was sixteen due to the color of yours."

"Whatever you say."

Cal rose from the machine, not happy with where the conversation was going. "Are you trying to make some kind of point here, Malcolm?"

Malcolm leaned in and his pectoral muscles swelled like balloons. "This isn't for common knowledge, but watching you back then helped me realize some things about my...inclinations."

"You mean you figured out you were gay?"

Malcolm stood and walked to the weight rack. "I don't like labels."

Cal couldn't resist. "Labels like 'closet gay'?"

Malcolm came face to face with Cal. "Take a breath, Cal. You're still the lord of the manor, but I'm no longer the poor, skinny kid who worked for your dad."

Cal reined in his emotions. "I appreciate that you're a part of Cozzi Cove's history."

"But not a part of *your* history? Or your present? Don't worry. I get it, Cal."

"And I appreciate you taking the time to help Michael with his career."

Malcolm smiled. "Michael's a nice boy." He looked Cal up and down. "And I've always had a soft spot for nice boys."

Cal locked into Malcolm's dark eyes. "Let me give you some advice. Stick to task with Michael."

"That's exactly what I plan to do."

"And by task I mean the magazine business."

Malcolm smiled. "I had the feeling."

Finished with his workout, Cal left the gym and drove back to Cozzi Cove. After parking his minivan, he walked into the main bungalow and found Michael still working at the desk in the front bedroom.

Standing in the doorway, he asked, "How's the article coming?"

"It's coming." Michael kept typing.

Cal entered the room and rested a hand on Michael's shoulder. "Can you take a break for a second?"

Michael looked up.

"Be careful with Malcolm."

Michael laughed. "Are you worried about what Taylor said last night?"

"Taylor's opinionated, egocentric, shortsighted, and bossy. But sometimes she's also right."

Michael went back to work on his laptop. "I told you I can take care of myself."

"Can you talk to me, please?"

Michael lowered the lid of his laptop and motioned for Cal to continue.

"I ran into Malcolm at the gym. The guy seems to have some kind of agenda."

"So do I." He stood up and wrapped his arms around Cal's waist. "I want a job to make my husband proud of me."

They shared a long kiss.

Michael fanned the air with his hands. "And I also want my husband to take a shower."

Cal backed off.

"And leave me alone so I can finish my article."

"Remember what I said about Malcolm." Cal kissed Michael's neck.

"Remember what I said about the shower."

Cal smiled and headed out the front porch onto the cove. He looked out at the pale blue sky dotted with marshmallow clouds reflecting on the calm bay water and thanked the gods for living in his own paradise. He threw off his tank top and ran into the bay. The warm ripples gently massaged his muscles as the sun bathed his body in golden light. As he swam toward the lighthouse in the distance, he imagined his great-grandfather at the cove as a young man in 1937 coming to terms with his sexuality. Standing in the shallow water, he gazed at the bungalows and envisioned his great-grandfather working on his heart's creation alongside the man he loved.

* * *

Billy Dean waved at Cal swimming in the bay. As he cleaned and restocked the six bungalows, he thought back to what had happened to him yesterday afternoon. Had it been a dream? A celestial vision? Was Jesus telling him it was okay to make love with someone? Or was the intimacy with Jesus and John symbolic of God's love for us all?

Billy Dean walked toward Bungalow Seven, located on a private strip of the cove, to finish his morning chores. When he'd cleaned number seven yesterday, the residents were already out, so Billy Dean had assumed, like him, they were early risers. However, when he knocked and announced, "Housekeeping," Jesus answered the door wearing a white bathrobe.

"Hi."

Billy Dean tottered back and forth unevenly on his feet. Jesus quickly took him by the arm to steady him and ushered him onto the glider on the front porch.

"Would you like some water?" Jesus asked.

Billy Dean nodded, unable to speak.

Jesus returned quickly with a glass of water. Billy Dean guzzled it down in one gulp.

John entered the porch wearing a similar bathrobe.

With the room spinning around him, Billy Dean croaked out, "Jesus and John."

"That's right." Jesus felt Billy Dean's pulse and rested a hand on his forehead. He said to John, "He doesn't have a fever. But his pulse is a bit elevated."

Billy Dean explained, "I was dizzy, but I'm all right now."

John smiled. "A big boy like you shouldn't feel dizzy. Did you eat breakfast?"

Billy Dean nodded. "Four hours ago."

"It could be a blood sugar issue," Jesus said.

"I'm a narcoleptic," Billy Dean explained. "And I've been missing my family and not sleeping well at night. So I drift off sometimes."

Jesus nodded. "Like you did yesterday."

"I hope you didn't mind us leaving you on the cove," John said. "You looked so peaceful that we didn't want to disturb you."

Billy Dean rested back on the glider, trying to put all the pieces of the puzzle together.

"You still look pale," Jesus said. "Come join us for breakfast on the patio."

A few moments later, the three of them were seated around the white oak table laden with poached eggs, vegetarian sausages, and fruit salad. Unable to eat, Billy Dean couldn't stop staring at Jesus and John.

"We didn't get your name yesterday," Jesus said to him.

"Billy Dean Boyd."

"I'm Jesus Santiago, and this is my partner John DeDeo."

John added, "Jesus is a nurse at the local hospital, and I'm a social worker at a local center for kids with developmental challenges. We're vacationing at Cozzi Cove this week."

"Given the maid's cart," Jesus said, "I'm guessing you're the new houseboy here."

"Did you know the houseboy before me?" Billy Dean asked after he was finally able to take a sip of grape juice.

Jesus and John grinned at each other. "Yeah, we knew Connor."

John added, "We were disappointed to hear he no longer worked at Cozzi Cove."

"Then we met you," Jesus said, followed by a wink.

"I'm a student at the local college, and I'm on the football team," Billy Dean said. "I'm here over the summer to rehearse the early fall college play. I just started working for Cal yesterday."

John gestured to the food. "Then you better eat up, Billy Dean. We don't want a big boy like you fainting on us."

Now that he'd accepted that Jesus and John were real people staying at Cozzi Cove and not biblical figures, Billy Dean filled his plate with food and ate heartily. "Since I zone out a lot due to my condition, I wasn't sure if yesterday really happened or was a dream."

"It really happened all right," Jesus said, followed by a pat on John's knee.

Billy Dean's face reddened. "I hope y'all don't think I'm 'dumber than a guy who falls in a barrel of titties and comes out sucking his thumb.' Something my grampa used to say."

Jesus and John smiled at him.

"But what happened on the cove yesterday—" Billy Dean chose his words carefully. "I thought—I mean since it was all like a vision—a part of me felt like—"

Jesus took his hand. "You can tell us, Billy Dean."

Billy Dean sighed. "I mean the way you were dressed...I thought you were the real Jesus and John." The two men stared at him blankly. "From the Bible."

Jesus and John shared a laugh and then Jesus explained, "We're in a group called the Angels. We wear white loincloths and angel wings and form a blockade when some evangelical groups picket the funerals of gay people and our allies."

"I'm a red-letter Christian. We'd never do something so hateful as picketing someone's funeral," Billy Dean said.

"I'm glad," John said. "We had just come from a funeral."

"And we'd left our wings in the van," Jesus added. "We saw you looking lost and adorable on the cove."

John added, "And when you said you wanted us, we couldn't resist."

"Are you in an open relationship?" Billy Dean asked.

Jesus took John's hand. "We only go with other people when we're together."

"How long have you two been together?" Bill Dean asked.

"We both grew up in Bayonne. Our parents were and still are best friends and neighbors." John smiled at Jesus. "So were we."

Jesus said, "We don't have any brothers or sisters. John and I became close early on. We've been a couple for twelve years. I couldn't imagine my life without him." He kissed John's forehead.

"And I wouldn't want to live without Jesus," John said, returning the kiss.

"But we've been best friends and lovers for so long, we decided a couple of years ago to share ourselves and our lives with others," Jesus said. "It started with a few of the Angels, but we expanded our horizons yesterday with you."

"I'm honored." Billy Dean thought the breakfast was one of the best he had ever eaten, including at his gramma's table. "I'm sure glad you shared your food with me too. This is amazing."

Jesus said, "We went to cooking school together in Bayonne."

"It must have been some school," Billy Dean said. "Usually I gulp down my food, but this is so good. I'm moving slower than molasses.'"

The three of them shared a smile, and then Jesus asked, "Where are you from, Billy Dean?"

"Mobile, Alabama."

"You come from a large family?" John asked.

Billy Dean washed down his food with juice. "Just my grampa, gramma, parents, three brothers, and two sisters." Nobody had ever listened to Billy Dean like this. Jesus and John seemed to really care about what he had to say.

Jesus asked, "How did your family feel when you moved North?"

Billy Dean started to wipe his mouth with his T-shirt, but John handed him a cloth napkin. "They were happy I got the football scholarship, and that I'd be near New York City, since I want to be on Broadway, and Alabama is pretty far from Broadway."

"That's for sure." They all laughed together.

More at ease, Billy Dean said, "What happened on the cove yesterday...was really nice."

"We enjoyed it too," John said.

"You seem like a very sweet young man," Jesus added.

"You guys were really gentle, and you made me feel relaxed and welcome," Billy Dean said.

"I'm glad," John said. "You seem quite in tune with your physical and spiritual sides, Billy Dean."

Jesus explained, "John and I are Buddhists."

"I've never met a Buddhist before," Billy Dean said.

"You have now." Jesus took John's hand.

"Does that mean you meditate and believe you have past lives?" Billy Dean asked.

Jesus nodded. "We also believe in peace, simple living, and doing good works in this life to build up rewards for the next."

The blood drained from Billy Dean's face. "Oh my God!"

"What is it?" Jesus asked, concerned.

"My pledge!"

"What pledge?" John asked.

Billy Dean's words came tumbling out of his mouth almost faster than his lips could form them. "Back home, I signed a virgin pledge card to honor Jesus with celibacy until I marry. I broke that promise on the cove last night with the both of y'all!" He leapt out of his seat as if it were on fire.

Jesus came to his feet quickly. "Billy Dean, I wouldn't get so upset."

"How can I not be upset!"

John stood and put a hand on Billy Dean's shoulder. "Take a few breaths, and we'll talk about it."

"I don't want to talk about it!" Tears streamed down Billy Dean's face. "I disobeyed the Lord with the both of y'all—who were like Eve's apple. And now I'm headed for the fires of Hell!" With that, Billy Dean ran out of the bungalow.

* * *

Nijad Hadad had just stepped out of Bungalow Five in a honey-colored polo shirt and navy-blue shorts, and he watched with curiosity as the houseboy raced out of Bungalow Seven. As Nijad approached the door of Bungalow Six, his thoughts shifted to Andrew and Annabel. Having not connected with anyone in such a long time, Nijad was shocked to find two people he liked. Both were attractive, engaging, intelligent, friendly, and good listeners. Where he found Annabel to be vivacious and a bit of a rebel, Andrew was warm and sweet. Like Nijad, they both loved to travel, and each sibling seemed to like him. He couldn't wait for their outing.

Andrew answered his knock on the door, wearing a violet short-sleeved shirt and tan shorts. "Nijad, I apologize for ducking out on you yesterday."

"Are you feeling better?"

Andrew nodded. "I'm more myself today." He opened the door and motioned for Nijad to come inside.

Entering the front porch, Nijad said, "Annabel and I had fun playing miniature golf yesterday. Actually, Annabel had fun. I was a sore loser."

Andrew laughed. "That's why I let Annabel play without me. She's a vixen at the game."

"Is she getting dressed?"

"Not exactly."

"Is something wrong?"

"No. Well, yes. I just left her lying in bed shaking her fist at me. It seems my illness wasn't food poisoning, but a twenty-four-hour bug I passed on to her."

"I'm sorry for Annabel. And glad you didn't pass it on to me." Nijad smiled.

"Good point. But after a day and night in bed, Annabel will be good as new. Take it from one who's been there."

"Should we cancel our plans?"

"Annabel said we should go without her, as long as I tell her everything that happened when I return."

"Sounds like a plan."

Nijad drove Andrew into town and parked in front of the diner. They went inside, sat at a booth near a window, and ordered chicken triple-decker sandwiches on eight-grain bread with sweet potato fries and coleslaw. The server brought their food, and they dug into the delicious but very filling lunches.

After a bit, Andrew smiled at Nijad and said, "It's nice to see you again."

Nijad again took in Andrew's handsome face. "This town is so quaint, and you're so welcoming. I feel as if I've gone back in time, or I'm in an alternate reality."

"Cozzi Cove is a magical place," Andrew said with a wink. "Besides, I can't imagine anyone being mean to someone as polite and friendly as you."

"My parents are soft-spoken, kind, and courteous. My brothers and I grew up that way. I went to small private schools, including college. It always surprises me when people are cruel, selfish, and discourteous."

Andrew took his hand. "You're a good man."

Nijad squeezed Andrew's hand. "Who is having lunch with another good man."

Andrew sat back in his seat. "I was raised very differently from you."

"I know. Annabel told me."

"My mother's mood swings were so severe, I didn't know whether to kiss her on the cheek or hide under the bed."

"Yet you and your sister turned out to be well-adjusted, successful, and, I admit, captivating people."

"Annabel got me through those dark days."

"She seems like quite a woman."

Andrew laughed. "Are you attracted to her?"

"Do you want the truth?"

"Of course."

Nijad smiled. "Actually, I'm attracted to both of you." He was surprised that Andrew seemed to enjoy his interest in Annabel.

Andrew leaned over and kissed Nijad and then pulled back. "I shouldn't have done that."

"Why not? I feel like a teenager necking in a diner booth. Not altogether a bad feeling." Nijad kissed Andrew. He wanted more. But, noticing some of the other patrons' eyes on them, they finished their lunches, paid the check, and left the diner.

Nijad and Andrew stopped at the candy store for saltwater taffy and ate the gooey, sweet wonders as they walked through the town, passing the bookstore, grocery store, flower shop, miniature golf center, Tommy Malone's bar, and Carla's Seafood Restaurant.

When they arrived at the trampoline emporium, Andrew took Nijad's arm. "Let's go in."

"After all we just ate?"

"We can use the exercise to work it off."

Andrew led Nijad inside and purchased two tickets. After walking through a long hallway, they found themselves outside gazing at a number of huge trampolines. Two little girls screamed as they jumped up and down on one of them. The others were vacant.

A tall, lanky teenage boy with acne all over his face put down his slice of pizza, took their tickets, and said, "Shoes off. Any open trampoline. You have thirty minutes."

After they took off their shoes, Andrew led Nijad atop a trampoline in the corner. Having never done this before, Nijad watched as Andrew jumped higher and higher, spinning in mid-air and laughing merrily. Andrew's movements caused Nijad to lose his balance.

"Join me!" Andrew said, out of breath.

Nijad leapt into the air and came down hard on his feet. That propelled him in the air even higher. Andrew took his hand, and they bounced together for a while. "Are you enjoying it?" Andrew asked.

"I feel like Peter Pan," Nijad said.

"Perfect! Cozzi Cove is Neverland, and I'm Michael."

"I guess that makes Annabel Wendy."

"Perfect!"

They bounced up and down until Nijad's stomach did a cartwheel. "I think I've had enough."

"It's near time to finish anyway," Andrew replied breathlessly.

"How do we stop?" Nijad asked, still bouncing.

"Like this." Andrew bounced in a sitting position, and Nijad followed him. Nijad accidentally fell on top of Andrew. They bounced that way with their arms around each other.

When they came to a stop still wrapped in each other's arms, Nijad said, "Do we have to move?"

Andrew laughed. "The young attendant will have to stop eating his pizza and come over here and scold us if we don't."

They leapt off the trampoline and left the emporium hand in hand. Walking through the park, they passed the statue of Cal Cozzi I, the gardens, and the small lake. When they arrived at the vacant children's play area, Andrew jumped onto one of the swings and swung higher and higher toward the white puffy clouds.

"You have an amazing constitution," Nijad said.

Andrew pumped his legs and called down to him, "Annabel can swing even higher."

"I'd like to see that."

"Maybe you will."

After Andrew finished swinging, they continued walking through the park until they came to a more secluded spot.

Nijad gazed at the sun bathing the cerulean sky and emerald trees in golden kisses. "I wish we could have dinner together tonight."

Andrew replied, "Me too."

"But you should probably stay with Annabel."

"I guess I should." They stopped in front of a waterfall cascading over steep rocks. "Are you disappointed?"

"Very. But I understand." Nijad took Andrew in his arms.

Andrew ran his hands over Nijad's mountainous shoulders, high-peaked biceps, wide pectoral muscles, and ripped abdominals. Then he kissed Nijad's prominent nose.

"Why did you do that?"

"I like your nose."

Nijad laughed. "I like your nose too." He kissed Andrew's button nose.

Andrew said, "I like everything about you."

Nijad kissed Andrew's full, juicy lips. "I like everything about you too." He lowered his hands down Andrew's lean back, and worked his way inside his pants to cup Andrew's smooth, round buttocks. They shared another kiss. "I don't want to stop."

"I don't either."

Nijad pressed his long, thick erection against Andrew's and kissed him harder on the mouth.

When a family of six walked close by them, Andrew pulled away. "We'd better get back."

Not letting it go, Nijad said, "After we return to Cozzi Cove, why don't you look in on Annabel and then come to my bungalow. If Annabel needs you, she can give you a call."

Andrew smiled and took Nijad's hand. "I'm flattered, but I think we should take this slowly."

"Why? We're both adults. And we're staying at the romantic Cozzi Cove."

Andrew sighed. "I've been hurt before when things didn't work out. I'm guessing you've been too. Let's take a good, long look before we leap."

"All right," Nijad said, as if his parent had just ruined his slumber party. "I'll continue looking. But I already like what I've seen so far."

"So do I."

They shared another long, wet kiss, and then left the park.

* * *

Billy Dean Boyd sat on the park bench, caught up in his own thoughts as Nijad and Andrew left, walking in front of him. Staring up at the bronze statue of Cal Cozzi's great-grandfather, Billy Dean thought the founder of Cozzi would no doubt have been a Christian, who, like his wife, had maintained his virginity until marriage. Unlike Billy Dean. Billy Dean had gotten down on his knees at the cove and prayed for forgiveness, but no word had come from the Lord. He had walked all over the town of Cozzi trying to calm down. Even though it summarized just how he was feeling, his grampa's old saying that he was "as jittery as two porcupines trying to make love" didn't give him comfort. With his head in his hands, Billy Dean repented for breaking his vow of chastity until marriage. He took the signed virgin card from his wallet and wept over it. Then he called out and begged for tender mercy, but none came. He recalled something else his grampa always said: "If you want to dance, you have to pay the fiddler."

"Here you are!"

Billy Dean looked up to at Jesus and John standing over him. He didn't know how he had ever mistaken them for anything else. Seeing them in their jeans and polo shirts, it was obvious they were mere mortals. "I'm sorry I ran out of your bungalow."

Jesus sat next to him. "We don't care about that."

John sat on Billy's Dean's other side. "We were worried about you."

"Y'all don't have to worry about me." Coming as he did from a large, poor family, and being strong and athletic since childhood, nobody had ever worried about Billy Dean before, except for his grampa when Billy Dean came home late.

"No we don't," Jesus said. "But we want to, because we care about you."

Billy Dean sighed. "How can y'all care about me? You hardly know me."

John took his hand. "We take seriously what we did at the cove. And we're hoping you'll be our friend."

"I don't have many friends."

"You've got two now."

"I'd like to be all y'all's friend too."

"Then it's settled. Let's go for a walk around town and talk things through," Jesus said.

Billy Dean rubbed his sore legs. "I walked from Cozzi Cove to here, and then I walked around town."

Jesus laughed. "Then let's sit here in the park and rest a while."

Billy Dean nodded and sat back. "I don't blame y'all for what happened at the cove. You didn't seduce me or anything. I wanted to do what we did. I wanted it very much. But now I have to face the consequences."

"What consequences?" John asked.

"Eternal damnation, like Cain faced for killing his brother Abel," Billy Dean replied.

John asked, "How many children did Adam and Eve have?"

"Two," Billy Dean replied. "Cain and Abel."

"Then where did Cain and Abel's wives come from?" John asked.

Billy Dean shrugged.

Jesus turned toward Billy Dean. "If there is an all-knowing creator, do you really think he, she, or they would create us to spend eternity in a fire pit?"

John rubbed his beard. "Besides, I don't recall Jesus talking about Hell."

"But He told the parable of the rich man having as much chance of getting into Heaven as a camel passing through the eye of a needle," Billy Dean replied.

"Christian conservatives have forgotten that passage. Maybe you should too." Jesus smiled. "Unless you're secretly rich."

"I'm definitely not rich," Billy Dean said.

"Maybe you are," John answered.

Billy Dean laughed with melancholy. "You think I have a fortune hidden in my maid's cart?"

"I think your fortune is hidden right here." John touched Billy Dean's chest.

"How come whenever you two guys touch me, it feels so relaxing?" Billy Dean asked.

"We studied Reiki," Jesus explained. "It's an ancient practice of touch used to relieve energy blockages."

"Is that why your hands are so warm?" Billy Dean asked.

John winked at him. "Warm hands, warm heart."

Jesus added, "We were practicing it on you at the cove." When he took Billy Dean's hand, it tingled. "You seem to be a kind, well-meaning, and gentle spirit. Why create a world in your mind of punishment and retribution?"

John rested a hand on Billy Dean's shoulder. "And remember, Jesus commanded people not to judge others. So why judge yourself?"

Billy Dean rubbed his forehead in confusion.

Jesus got up from the bench and pulled Billy Dean up with him. "Come on, young man. We're going to drive you back to Cozzi Cove. While you do turndown service, we'll make dinner. Please come as our guest."

"I have play rehearsal until nine o'clock," Billy Dean said.

"We'll wait dinner for you," John replied.

Billy Dean sure liked their cooking. "All right."

"Good. Come with us."

Billy Dean followed Jesus and John out of the park, wondering if his fate would be the same as the disciples of yore.

CHAPTER SIX

That evening after leaving the Horror Convention, Jonathan Harper went to the grocery store in town and then drove back to Cozzi Cove. After entering his bungalow, he petted Renfield and headed for the kitchen, where he prepared lamb chops—rare for Vlad—whole wheat macaroni and cheese, and creamed spinach. He was careful not to use parsley or garlic, recalling Vlad's allergy. Renfield followed at Jonathan's heels as he went outside to set the white oak patio table for two and placed two dog dishes underneath it. Then Jonathan hurried back into the bungalow to the front bedroom and put on tan slacks and a cerise-colored polo shirt that reflected a bit of color onto his pale, sunken cheeks.

Hearing a knock at the door, Jonathan hurried to the front porch with Renfield close behind him. When Jonathan opened the door to Vlad, Renfield stood at attention, locking eyes with the guest. With the agility of a twenty-year-old, Vlad kneeled and petted Renfield. Then Renfield played the role of host and led Vlad's dog Barnabas through the house to the backyard. Vlad rose to his feet quickly and handed Jonathan a bouquet of blood-red roses. "For my host."

Jonathan blushed. "They're really nice. Thank you." He brought them up for a sniff and cut his finger on a thorn. Dark red blood covered his index finger.

Vlad's eyes widened, and he focused only on Jonathan's finger. "Let me take care of that for you." Vlad rested the flowers on an end table, hurried Jonathan through the living room into the bathroom, turned on the faucet, and placed Jonathan's finger under it. After drying off Jonathan's finger with a hand towel, he rummaged in a cabinet drawer, took out a medicated bandage, and covered the finger. "I'm sorry for the thorn."

"I'll live. Thank you for taking care of it. If acting doesn't work out, you might try a career as a nurse."

They smiled at each other. Jonathan realized Vlad was still holding his hand. He was enjoying it too much to break the contact.

Finally, Vlad released Jonathan's hand. Then with the grace of a dancer, he swept back onto the front porch, scooped up the flowers, and walked with Jonathan out the back kitchen door to the patio, where Renfield and Barnabas were already enjoying their dinners under the table.

Vlad artfully placed the flowers with others already in the vase on the table. Jonathan couldn't take his eyes off Vlad's broad shoulders, framed nicely by his stylish black tunic, nor his narrow hips and long, lean legs encased in tailored white slacks.

They sat at the table across from each other. Vlad looked down at the goblets filled with red wine and the plates full of delicious-looking food. "My mouth is watering."

Jonathan's mouth was watering too, but not for the food.

"I'm absolutely starving," Vlad said.

"No wonder. You worked hard today at the convention."

"Thank you for noticing. And thank you for dinner."

"My pleasure."

They toasted and drank their wine.

"How was my Dracula performance at the convention?"

"Terrific. I'm a believer. Especially after I researched your lineage."

Vlad picked up his knife and fork and tore into his blood-rare lamb chops. "What did you find out?"

Bursting to tell Vlad, Jonathan slid to the edge of his seat. "I entered all of your information onto the web site."

"How much did that cost?"

"Fifty dollars."

"Hey, I'm a starving actor!"

"It's my treat."

"I'm liking this lineage thing more and more." Vlad gave him a huge grin, and Jonathan couldn't help noticing Vlad's large molars.

Jonathan rubbed his hands together like a witch about to cast a spell. "I found out your ancestry traces back to Alba Iulia!"

"Is that a good thing?"

Jonathan's jaw dropped. "It's an *amazing* thing!"

"Why?" Having finished both his lamb chops, Vlad moved on to the side dishes.

"Alba Iulia is a city in central Romania!"

"Okay?"

"And Alba Iulia is located in the region of Ardeal, or Transylvania. The very same region where Prince Vlad III, the Impaler, the Prince of Wallachia, of the House of Draculesti lived in a decaying castle in the Carpathian Mountains near the Borgo Pass in the fifteenth century!"

"So?"

"So the life of Prince Vlad III inspired Bram Stoker to write *Dracula* in the late nineteenth century. Don't you get it?" Jonathan's heart was racing. He couldn't stop himself from talking a mile a minute. "Your unusual strength for someone so slender, your youthful agility and hypnotic power over animals, your lack of shadow at night on the cove, the love you have for bloody meat, the giant molars in your mouth, your dislike of the sun, the allergy to garlic, and the ease with which you twirl your cape and bite people on the neck. It all adds up!"

Vlad's jaw dropped. "Are you saying you think I'm a real vampire?"

Jonathan pushed his plate away. "I'm saying I believe you are a descendant of a real vampire. And through the generations, the vampire traits may have remained and mutated into your genes."

"So you think I'm a mini vampire?"

Jonathan moved quickly to his feet and paced the patio. "I believe you've inherited some of the traits and powers of your ancestor Prince Vlad III. I witnessed some of them myself. As to any others, perhaps you've subconsciously suppressed them due to your fear of them, or lack of knowledge on how to use them?"

Having finished his dinner, Vlad moved to Jonathan's side. "Are you telling me I should sleep in a coffin during the day and suck people's blood at night?"

"Not yet."

Vlad did a double take.

"I think you should consider what I found out. Explore the side of you that you've yet to embrace. Open yourself up to the possibility, and see if your vampire traits and powers can be reawakened and cultivated."

"I'm a method actor, but this is taking things a bit too far."

"But don't you want to get to know who you really are?"

"I know who I am. Vlad Lesti, a fifty-year-old actor who lives hand to mouth in New York City."

Jonathan tented his fingers. "My point exactly!"

Vlad scratched at his long hair. "You lost me."

"Think about it, Vlad. If you really have some of Dracula's genes, and you embrace them, the press will be at your door. And if the press is at your door, film and TV offers will follow."

"I don't want to be a freak TV reality actor."

"No. But wouldn't you like to star in your own television show, where you play a vampire?"

"Of course."

"This could be just the thing to get producers to notice."

Vlad rubbed his strong chin, considering it. Finally, he said, "I see your point. We do live in a tabloid world."

Jonathan breathed a sigh of relief. "So why not take advantage of it?"

"All right. Let's give it a try." Vlad faced Jonathan. "What do you think I should do to awaken the hidden vampire in me?"

"Let's start with Renfield and Barnabas," Jonathan replied. "Think about something you want them to do. See if your thought waves can penetrate theirs. Will them to obey your command."

Vlad shrugged and walked over to the two dogs. He knelt at their side, and they locked eyes with his. Lines appeared on Vlad's smooth forehead. Suddenly, the dogs leapt onto him and licked his cheeks.

"Is that what you wanted them to do?" Jonathan asked, excited.

"I willed them to stand," Vlad replied. He signaled the dogs to return under the table, and stood up.

"And they did!" Jonathan stood next to Vlad. "When they licked your cheeks."

"Are you sure they didn't lick me because I kneeled next to them, and they smelled the lamb chops on my breath?"

Jonathan placed a hand on his hip. "They did as you mentally commanded, because your ancestor Prince Vlad III, aka Count Dracula, had hypnotic power over animals, and you have some of his genes."

"But can't Dracula also appear and disappear? I've never accomplished that trick."

"Baby steps." Jonathan pulled off his bandage. "Look at my finger."

Vlad obeyed.

"Gaze at the blood on the bandage."

Again Vlad did as Jonathan asked.

"What are you thinking?"

"That the bleeding has stopped. So you must be healing. I'm glad."

Jonathan groaned. "Stop thinking about me. Focus on the blood."

Vlad took the bandage in his hand and stared at it.

"How does it make you feel?"

Vlad replied, "Like asking for your lamb chop if you aren't going to eat it."

Jonathan sighed and took back the bandage. "Does the blood on the bandage make you...desirous?"

"Why would I desire dried up blood?"

"Good point."

Jonathan put the bandage back on his finger and stood closer to Vlad. "Look at my neck."

Vlad focused on Jonathan's neck.

"How does it seem to you?"

"Nice."

"Now we're getting somewhere. Why does it look nice?"

Vlad focused on Jonathan's neck. "Because it's pale and soft, and it's yours."

"Mine?"

He looked at Jonathan. "You're a nice guy. I like you."

Jonathan tilted Vlad's head back to focus on his neck. "Stare at my neck and don't look away." After a few moments, Jonathan said, "There's nothing in the world other than your mouth and my neck."

"This is weird, Jonathan."

"You're an actor for goodness sake. Pretend this is an acting exercise."

"All right." Vlad stared at Jonathan's neck.

Jonathan said softly, "Your mouth and my neck. What do you want to do, Vlad?"

"Eat your lamb chops."

"What else?"

"Eat your mac and cheese?"

"Concentrate, Vlad."

Vlad swayed a bit to one side.

"What is it?"

"Something's happening."

"Go with it, Vlad. Do what your impulses and your genetic makeup are commanding you to do." Jonathan couldn't hide his excitement over the possibility of being bitten by a real vampire.

Suddenly, Vlad sucked in air, bent down, and kissed Jonathan's neck. Then he grasped Jonathan's head in his hands and pressed his lips against Jonathan's mouth. They shared a long kiss. When Vlad released him, Jonathan panted in shock.

"I have to go," Vlad said, as if seeing a ghost. He headed quickly for the kitchen door with Barnabas close at his heels.

Jonathan and Renfield followed them through the kitchen and living room and onto the front porch. "Wait! Vlad!"

Vlad yanked open the front door. "I'm sorry." And he and Barnabas fled to the bungalow next door.

Jonathan closed his door and sat on the porch rocking chair. As he petted Renfield at his feet, he smiled.

* * *

Billy Dean walked along the cove and waved to Jonathan Harper sitting on his front porch. He hadn't enjoyed his play rehearsal that evening. It wasn't the singing, dancing, and acting that bothered him. That part was fine. His heart just wasn't in it as he could only think about his broken promise. As he walked along the cove, he took his virgin card out of his wallet, tore it in half, and threw it in a garbage can.

His stomach was growling when he reached the door to Bungalow Seven. Billy Dean also had to admit that it wasn't just the dinner that enticed him. He liked being with Jesus and John.

Billy Dean knocked on the door, and Jesus answered, offering him a big smile. "We've been waiting dinner for you. Come on in."

A few minutes later, Billy Dean, Jesus, and John sat on the patio enjoying a feast of spinach and artichoke dip, red lentils and beet salad, pumpkin and butternut squash soup, roasted wild mushrooms, quinoa and grilled vegetables, chickpea and eggplant tarts, vegetable shepherds' pie, and four-berry shortcake for dessert.

"This is the best food I've ever eaten," Billy Dean said.

"Better than college cafeteria food?" John asked with a wink.

Billy Dean nodded. "Even better than my gramma's. And probably a lot healthier than her fried chicken, grits in butter, and biscuits and gravy." He finished his plate and made himself another. "Are y'all vegetarians?"

Jesus nodded. "That's part of the Buddhist lifestyle. We don't harm or kill any life form, including animals."

"Y'all wouldn't fit in too well in Alabama. My daddy gave me my first hunting rifle when I was eight."

"Did you kill a lot of animals?" Jesus asked.

"Just a few bucks, some turkeys, and a bear."

When Jesus and John looked at each other in horror, Billy Dean changed the subject and asked about their day.

Jesus and John talked about being off work during the week and attending another funeral that afternoon to act as shields with the Angels. Then John asked, "How was your day?"

"Fine." Billy Dean looked down at the ground.

"Are you feeling any better?" Jesus said.

"Not really. But please don't think I'm ungrateful. I enjoyed what we did at the cove. I mean I *really* enjoyed it. But I still have this guilty feeling I can't shake off." Billy Dean finished his second plate.

Jesus stood. "How about we show you some Reiki? It might make you feel better."

"That would be great."

John rose and placed Billy Dean between them.

Jesus placed his hand over Billy Dean's chest without touching it. "Do you feel that?"

Billy Dean nodded. "It's all tingly."

"In Reiki we learn to summon up our own energy, so we can share it with others." John hovered his hand over Billy Dean's head. "How's that?"

"Amazing, and y'all didn't even touch me!" Billy Dean said.

"We don't have to," Jesus explained.

Suddenly, Billy Dean's guilt was replaced with desire. "It's so muggy outside, I feel stickier than honey on a biscuit." Billy Dean threw off his T-shirt and shorts, turned on the hot tub, and adjusted the heat setting upward. Then he leapt into the tub and stood with the bubbles surrounding him. "It's really refreshing. Take off your clothes and come on in and join me, y'all."

Jesus and John did as Billy Dean asked.

Billy Dean stood between Jesus and John. "My grampa would say we're 'cozier than three fleas in a dog's ear.'" He kissed Jesus slowly and passionately, and then he turned and did the same with John.

"Are you sure this is what you want?" Jesus asked.

"I've never been more certain of anything in my whole life," Billy Dean said.

John added, "We don't want you to do something that might upset you."

"I'm not upset. I'm on fire!" Billy Dean replied.

When Jesus moved behind Billy Dean and placed his hands on Billy Dean's broad shoulders, an electric charge ran through him. Then, as Jesus massaged the rippling muscles on his back, Billy Dean sighed and relaxed in the warm bubbling water as the knots melted away. Jesus then worked his way down to Billy Dean's round, firmly muscled buttocks.

Standing in front of Billy Dean, John placed his hands on Billy Dean's chest. It was as if satin were caressing his wide pectoral muscles. John continued stroking down to Billy Dean's firm six-pack abdominals.

Still behind him, Jesus turned his head gently, and kissed him tenderly. John leaned over and did the same.

Billy Dean rested back against Jesus's chest, and the amazing sensations flowed through him like shock waves.

John went to his knees and massaged the muscles in Billy Dean's thighs and calves. Then he kissed and licked his patch of blond pubic hair. As he cupped Billy Dean's low-hanging testicles, John took him in his mouth and rolled his tongue around Billy Dean's thick shaft and even thicker head. Finally, he pressed his index finger deep inside Billy Dean's hole, and Billy Dean cried out in ecstasy. After a few moments, John stood back up to capture Billy Dean's mouth in a wet kiss.

Still massaging Billy Dean's back muscles, Jesus gently pushed him down until Billy Dean was bent over, facing John's long, slender cock surrounded by jet-black pubic hair.

John gently cupped the back of Billy Dean's head and pulled him forward. Billy Dean grasped onto John's firm buttocks and did to John what had been done to him. John moaned in delight and appreciation as he massaged the back of Billy Dean's neck.

Jesus reached onto the deck for a lubed condom and slipped it on. He then gently entered Billy Dean from behind. Billy Dean pulled off of John and screamed out at first in pain and then in elation as Jesus thrust his thick pole in and out, all the while massaging Billy Dean's back, buttocks, and thighs. Then Jesus took hold of Billy Dean's dick and rubbed very slowly and softly, building gradually in intensity and speed.

Still holding on to John's smooth buttocks, Billy Dean let out a thrilled cry of delight and fulfillment as he shot into the hot tub.

A moment later, John came all over Billy Dean's face, and Jesus did the same on Billy Dean's back. Then the three of them kissed and cuddled.

When they had all caught their breaths, Jesus asked, "Feel better?"

Billy Dean replied, his voice languid, "I haven't felt this good in a long time. I tell you one thing, y'all can suck the chrome off a trailer hitch."

Jesus and John looked at each other and burst out laughing. Billy Dean joined them, and the three of them laughed in each other's arms.

A little tickle was born in Billy Dean's lower stomach that built and grew in intensity and speed like a tiny white light turning into a floodlight. Billy Dean had tasted a bit of heaven on earth, and he was ready for paradise.

He led Jesus and John into the house to the front bedroom. Billy Dean stretched out on the bed, his arms around Jesus and John, as he lay on top of them. As the three men kissed and cuddled, the loneliness, angst, and fear inside Billy Dean finally released. He kissed and licked Jesus from his forehead to his toes. He did the same to John. Then Billy Dean took Jesus's dick in his mouth. That propelled Jesus to do the same with John, and John to follow suit with Billy Dean. The three of them kissed, licked, and sucked until Billy Dean was ready to explode.

John then put on a lubed condom, gently turned Billy Dean onto his back and, pushing his knees back, entered Billy Dean from above him. Jesus, facing John, carefully went to his knees over Billy Dean's head. Billy Dean took Jesus into his mouth, sucking, licking, and nibbling first on his testicles and then his thick, hook-shaped dick. Above him, Jesus and John shared a deep kiss as they each thrust gently into Billy Dean.

Just before Billy Dean was ready to orgasm, Jesus gently pulled Billy Dean up onto his knees and slipped a lubed condom on him. Jesus then turned around and kneeled in front of him. As Billy Dean entered Jesus from behind, John placed a condom on Jesus, turned around, and kneeled in front of him. Jesus penetrated John quickly. Billy Dean and Jesus started slowly and then built up to quicker and stronger thrusts. Billy Dean kissed Jesus's back and wrapped his arms around Jesus and John. They both reached back for Billy Dean. When Billy Dean couldn't hold off a moment longer, they switched positions with John inside Jesus and Jesus inside Billy Dean.

Finally, Jesus and John tore off their condoms and the three men lay on their backs on the bed with Billy Dean in the middle. Billy Dean clutched Jesus and John's dicks, and they grasped his. Billy Dean shot first with a shout of joy and euphoria. Jesus was next with John following. In the afterglow, the three men lay in each other's arms, kissing and hugging until sleep overtook them.

* * *

Shortly before midnight, Cal walked past Bungalow Seven and headed down the cove. A walk along the cove always centered Cal. He wondered how different it might have looked during his great-grandfather's time.

Arriving at the main bungalow, Cal let himself onto the porch and headed to the front bedroom, where he found Michael asleep in their bed with his laptop resting on top of him. Cal quietly put Michael's laptop on the desk, slipped off his clothes, got into bed, and turned on the pin light atop his night table. Then, taking his great-grandfather's diary from the night table, he opened to the next entry.

June 12, 1937.

My assistant and I finished laying down the foundation for the main bungalow at Cozzi Cove today. That's where I will live with my mother and my son. We are moving on now to lay down the foundation for the seven guest bungalows. Since each bungalow will be exactly the same, and the concrete, metal, bricks, stone, and waterproofing materials have been delivered, we should move pretty quickly now. I took my mother and my son to the site yesterday. Mama cried thinking about Daddy. Calvin Jr. giggled and clapped his hands. I could tell he really liked it. That's good since he will inherit it all one day.

I found out my assistant is a bit of a young hothead. My ground plan has the front door of each bungalow leading from a screened-in porch to a sitting room and then a kitchen. The first bedroom is off the living room, and the second bedroom is off the kitchen. The bathroom is between the second bedroom and kitchen. So, from the front porch, sitting room, and front bedroom, our guests will be able to see the cove. My assistant thought up a different plan, where the windows of all the rooms could open to the cove. But it allowed for only three guest cottages instead of seven. When I pointed that out, he threw down his cap, jumped into his old Ford, and took an early lunch. After he cooled down, he came back and worked harder than ever.

Each night when the sun goes down, we would stop working and head over to Mangione's Seafood Restaurant for dinner caught fresh from the ocean. Over seafood chowder, scallops, shrimp, salmon, sole, or flounder, with creamy potatoes and coleslaw, we would talk about everything in our heads. Even though he is younger than me, we think the same about most things. We both hope President Roosevelt will get to serve a third term, or even a fourth term if he wants one. Fish is our favorite food. We love working with our hands. And sea air, sand, and salt water are in our veins and hearts. After we finish building Cozzi Cove, we have some great ideas on how to build some things in town— like a row of stores near the park, more places for cars to park near the beach, and roads to connect everything. He says if we do all that, they will put a statue of me in the park and rename the town after me. I have to admit I would really like that. I also admit I really like him, and I think he really likes me. While that tickles me, it also scares me. Obviously, nobody can know we like each other, or we would be called "queers" and run out of town. That's why I am not writing his name in my diary. Just in case anyone ever finds it. I would not want my friend to suffer for what I needed to write.

I first knew I was different at ten years old. My aunt and her family came to visit us from Delaware one summer. While our mothers sewed in the kitchen and our fathers smoked cigars in the sitting room, my male cousin and I would go to the beach to make sandcastles, catch seashells, climb up onto the rocks, and swim in the waves. He was three years older than me, athletic, with carrot red hair and freckles all over. I had the time of my life with him. I remember us diving in and out of the waves. One time a big wave knocked me down. As the undertow carried me into the sea, my cousin swam over, put my arms around his neck, and swam me to shore on his back. I had never felt so warm and protected before. That night, we made a bonfire at the beach and cuddled together under my mama's old blanket. He smelled like the sea, and I liked it when his strong, bare chest rubbed against mine. I nearly burst through my breeches when he told me he liked me, and he put his arm around me. Since we shared my bed back at our house, we continued cuddling all night. My mama caught us the next morning, and she told my father. My cousin and I overheard our parents talking with serious voices. I cried when my cousin and his family left. I cried even louder when my father gave me a whooping with his belt. They never visited us again.

When I am on the beach, I enjoy watching the men in their bathing suits more than the women. All through school, I felt the same way about the boys. I even fooled around some with my classmates in the bathroom. But I never went too far, knowing what getting caught would have done to my family.

I did not have a girl in high school or at Sunday school. My mama got concerned and introduced me to the daughter of one of the women in her sewing circle. Gertrude was pretty, funny, and smart. She was a great cook and sewed pretty clothes, tablecloths, and curtains. She also spent most of her time giggling with her girlfriend, Trudy, which was fine by me. When Mama kept asking us about it, we got married and had a baby. I was thrilled beyond words to have a son. But I was sure sorry when Gertrude passed away. She would have loved raising Calvin Jr. I still miss her, but I cannot say I ever loved her, or that she ever loved me.

I do not think I ever experienced love until building Cozzi Cove. My assistant is stirring something up inside me that is thrilling, bewildering, and terrifying. When he compliments how I look, disagrees with me about construction, cocks his head and pushes out his lower lip, or gazes at me with adoration, I have to hold myself back from pushing him down on the concrete, taking him in my arms, pressing my lips against his, and reaching down under his breeches for his manhood. I have prayed about this. I have been praying about it since I was ten years old. No help has come. At least not yet. I sure hope the Lord answers my prayers soon. I do not think I can hold myself back much longer. I have a suspicion my friend feels the same way.

CHAPTER SEVEN

The next afternoon, Michael Rodgers knocked on the door of Bungalow Two. He was wearing his best navy dress shirt and gray slacks, and carried his laptop in his shaking hand.

Malcolm Wolf opened the door wearing a lavender Speedo. He gestured to the glider on the front porch. "Welcome, Michael. Let's sit out here and enjoy the amazing view."

Michael entered and took a seat, happy to get off his wobbly legs. "Thank you again for agreeing to look at my work, Malcolm. I really appreciate it."

"Wait until you hear my critique. You may not appreciate that." Malcolm winked at him and then sat next to Michael on the glider. "Let's see what we've got here, young man." He placed the laptop on the end table.

Michael opened the file as sweat dripped down his back. As he gazed out at the clear bay water tickling the rocks, he would sneak looks at Malcolm's expression as the senior editor examined the photographs for the article. Malcolm never altered his focus, and his face didn't give away what he was thinking.

After what seemed like an eternity, Malcolm leaned back on the glider.

"What do you think?" Michael held his breath.

"It needs work."

Michael's heart stopped beating.

"But it also has a great deal of merit."

Michael exhaled and rejoined the living. "Thank you, Malcolm."

"Don't thank me. Thank yourself. You created a good story with photographs that are stimulating and carry a great deal of subtext."

Michael basked in the compliments, and then took in a deep breath to brace himself for a dose of reality. "What doesn't work in the article?"

Malcolm leaned in toward the laptop. "This shot."

In order to see it, Michael had to gaze over Malcolm's mountainous shoulder past his wide muscled chest.

Malcolm pressed his shoulder against Michael's as he examined the photograph. "This tells a different story from the other shots."

"How so?"

"The guy's too soft looking."

"What's wrong with that?"

"Readers might think it's a gay article. And you already have a picture of a black guy. If half your pictures are of black dudes, the readers might think it's a black article." Malcolm stretched his arm around the back of the glider. "Did you have the guys in the pictures sign a release form?"

"No. I was so busy getting the article done, I didn't think of that. Plus, I didn't think the article was for publication."

"With the web being at everyone's disposal, anything should be considered possible for publication. And when I give you a critique, don't come back with excuses. It wastes your time and mine. Just listen and learn for next time. Got it?"

Michael nodded.

Malcolm rested his hand on Michael's shoulder, and Michael smelled his coconut-scented lotion. "As I expected, you are a young man with great potential and talent."

"Thank you."

"I'm proud of you." Malcolm hugged Michael to his chest.

While Michael enjoyed Malcolm's strong chest pressed against his and Malcolm's strong arms around him, he was uncomfortable with the editor's physical display of affection.

Malcolm released Michael. "When I was your age, I wished I had someone to help me and guide me."

Michael rose and then picked up the laptop. "And I'm really grateful for your help and guidance." He moved toward the front door. "I'll make the changes on the article and e-mail it to you before I leave for work later this afternoon."

"Not so fast. There's a great deal left for you to learn about this business."

"I'm willing to do that."

"Are you?"

Michael nodded.

Malcolm stood up opposite Michael near the front door. "Good. Because I'd like to take on the role of your mentor."

"I'm honored."

"My time is quite valuable, and I offer it infrequently, but something tells me you're worth it. Are you worth it, Michael?"

"I hope so."

"So do I. I don't work well over the phone or e-mail. I like personal contact. So it'll mean that we get together from time to time in New York."

"I can drive into the city."

"All right. Then I have a few calls to make and some thinking to do."

"About what?"

"About you." Malcolm leaned his arm against the door, causing his bicep to graze Michael's cheek.

Michael couldn't pretend he didn't enjoy the sensation, but it frightened him at the same time.

"I need to speak to some of my staff members to see if we have an opening for you. I can't promise anything. And if I have something, it will be an entry-level position."

"Are you serious?"

Malcolm's minty breath wafted over him. "I'm very serious."

"That's terrific!"

"Let's see what comes up."

"Thank you. Thank you so much, Malcolm!" Michael left the bungalow on cloud nine. He sprinted across the cove and into the main bungalow. Barely able to keep his feet on the bamboo floor, he stood before Cal who was working at his desk in the living room.

Cal rose and walked around the desk toward Michael. "I'm guessing Malcolm liked the article."

Michael nodded. "Not only that, he wants to be my mentor!"

A line formed across Cal's forehead. "How will that work?"

"I'll go into the city occasionally to meet with him. I'm guessing he'll go over my articles, give me some tips about the business, and maybe even some advice on eventually becoming an editor like him. *And* Malcolm has to talk to some people first, but he may have a job for me!" Michael kissed Cal. Then he ran into the front bedroom.

Cal followed him. "What are you doing?"

Michael sat at the desk and turned on his laptop. "Making a few changes in the article. And I need to take a picture of you."

"Of *me*?"

"Malcolm doesn't like one of my pictures because the guy's black and looks gay."

"What's wrong with black gay people?"

"Nothing, except you don't want too many or the readers will think it's about that. So I need to replace it with a photo of a butch white guy. And I need you to sign a release form."

"Stating I'm a butch white guy?"

"Giving me permission to use your picture in the article."

"Where are you going to post the article?"

"Nowhere. It's just a formality."

Cal rested his hands on Michael's shoulders. It always made Michael feel grounded. "Are you sure working with Malcolm is the right thing for you?"

"Positive!" Michael typed as he talked. "Malcolm doesn't offer his time to just anybody. He thinks I'm really talented."

"Then maybe you should wait for an editor whose goals and interests match yours more fully."

"I've had my resume online forever. Nobody's interested." Michael kissed Cal's hand. "Except for Malcolm Wolf! And that is fine by me. Hurry up and change into your bathing suit."

"Yes, sir." Cal saluted and went to the bureau to change into his aqua trunks.

Michael picked up his camera, and he and Cal headed outside. Michael took pictures of Cal next to a tall cobalt rock on the white sand. When he had the picture he wanted, he hurried inside to save the file to his computer and replace the old picture with the new one. He then did a little more editing and e-mailed the revised article to Malcolm, hurried outside to kiss Cal at the cove, ran to the parking lot, and drove off to Tommy's bar.

* * *

As Nijad Hadad exited his bungalow in a raspberry polo shirt and tan shorts, he noticed Cal Cozzi heading for the main bungalow. Nijad took in a deep breath and enjoyed the antics of the bay water fondling the jagged rocks. As he looked out at the old lighthouse taking center stage against the Maya-blue sky, Annabel approached and stood next to him.

"You look as if you're solving the problems of the world."

Nijad couldn't help smiling at the Annabel, who looked stunning in a strawberry-colored sundress and sunhat. "Are you feeling better?"

"One day and night lying on my arse in bed did the trick."

They shared a smile.

"What are your plans for today?" Nijad asked.

"Anything that doesn't involve a loo, a bed, or a telly."

"May I take you and Andrew to lunch?"

"Follow me." Annabel led Nijad into her bungalow through the porch. As they passed it, Nijad peeked into the front bedroom, which Andrew kept tidy with everything in its place. Once again, Annabel's rear bedroom looked like a brothel after an earthquake. Upon entering the kitchen, Annabel scooped up a plate, glass, napkin, and utensils and then led him through the rear door onto the coral stone patio.

As she set a second place at the white oak table, Nijad asked, "Are you and your brother having lunch al fresco?"

"Andrew is getting a haircut. The second place setting is for you."

"I don't want to intrude."

"You aren't. It's more fun eating with someone than eating alone, isn't it?"

"Thank you."

"My pleasure."

Nijad sat on a white wicker chair opposite Annabel. She served them scallops with avocado tomato basil salad, and poured iced tea. After tasting the food, Nijad smiled. "You're a very good cook."

"Andrew made it before he left."

"Lucky us."

Though lunch tasted delicious, Nijad couldn't stop staring at Annabel's beauty. "You're no longer sick."

"How do you know?"

"You have your color back."

"Lovely."

"That you are." As he helped himself to brown bread and butter, he asked, "Now that you both live together again, does Andrew do most of the cooking?"

"Thankfully, yes. He always did. When we were children, he even made the biscuits for our tea parties."

"Where did he learn to cook?"

"Andrew can learn anything by reading a book. I'm much more tactile."

Nijad couldn't stop himself from thinking how much he'd like to be tactile with Annabel.

"I heard you two 'bounced around' Cozzi yesterday."

Nijad laughed. "Andrew bounced. I buoyed."

Annabel's eyes softened. "And you shared a kiss."

"Andrew told you?"

She nodded. "Does that bother you?"

"No. But it presents a bit of a dilemma for me."

Annabel raised an eyebrow.

"I've always believed in truthful relationships and monogamy."

"You mean you have to decide which of us to shag?"

Nijad couldn't believe how different the brother and sister were in terms of romance. Where Andrew was shy, ponderous, and reticent, Annabel seemed adventurous, spontaneous, and daring. "If you are both interested in having a relationship with me, I'll need to make a decision."

"There are some things you don't know about Andrew and me."

"Such as?"

After taking a swallow of her iced tea, Annabel said, "My brother and I have never been competitive. When I'm happy, he's happy, and vice versa. As kids, when our mum was out for blood, I'd protect Andrew. When he wasn't fast enough to get away from her, I'd take the beatings for him, or let him cry in my arms. As twins, we're very closely connected. So we won't be at odds over you."

"I'm glad to hear that." Nijad finished his lunch. "I wouldn't want to cause any trouble or ill feelings between you."

"I'm perfectly willing to step aside if it's Andrew you prefer. Andrew is willing to do the same if it's me who piques your interest."

"I'm glad there is no jealousy between you."

"That would never happen." She giggled. "I'd even consider sharing you, if that's what you and Andrew fancy."

It was like being a guest at a buffet with too many options. "I'll have to carefully consider that one." Having finished his lunch, Nijad wiped his mouth with the napkin. "Well, thank you again. It was delicious. Would you like to go for a walk on the cove?"

"I'm still a tad buggered. I probably should have eaten something a bit lighter. But I never like to deny myself anything."

Nijad liked the sound of that.

"Let's sit in the living room."

Nijad followed Annabel from the warm patio into the air-conditioned bungalow, through the kitchen to the living room. When they were seated comfortably on the sofa, gazing out at the cove, Nijad said, "When the time comes, I won't want to leave Cozzi Cove."

"Cheers to that."

Nijad rested his arm on the back of the sofa and then slid it about Annabel's shoulders. "This is nice."

Annabel lay her head on Nijad's shoulder. "Mm-hmm."

"Do you feel better?"

"Quite."

Unable to stop himself, Nijad lifted her chin and pressed his lips over hers. They shared a long, wet, sensuous kiss. He wrapped his arms around her, and she did the same, massaging the vast muscles in his back. After more kissing, Annabel pushed him away. "Am I moving too fast?"

"I'm still a bit queasy," she said, holding her stomach.

He sat up. "Can I make you some tea?"

"No. I'll be all right."

Not wanting to wear out his welcome, Nijad rose. "I should let you get your rest."

Annabel walked him to the front porch. "I'm sure I'll be myself by tomorrow."

"Then tomorrow it is. Would you like to go to the main beach?"

"That would be smashing!"

"How about if I pick you and Andrew up at one?"

"One it is."

They stopped at the front door. "I'm really looking forward to it."

"Me too."

Nijad took Annabel in his arms and kissed her lightly on the forehead. When she seemed to want more, he pressed her against him and kissed her more forcefully on the mouth. Just like when he'd kissed Andrew, Nijad's erection pressed against Andrew's erection. But Annabel shouldn't have an erection. Nijad pulled the top of Annabel's blouse toward him and glared down at the bra stuffed with padding.

He stepped back and banged into the front door. "You're Andrew!"

Andrew's face flushed. "I can explain."

Nijad pulled off the wig and threw it at Andrew. "You're trying to make a fool of me."

"No!"

"Because I'm bisexual, you mocked me by pretending to have a sister!"

"It's not what you think." Tears filled Andrew's eyes.

"What else can it be? You can play your dress up games without me." Nijad yanked the door open and stormed out of the bungalow.

"Nijad, wait!"

He hurried into the bungalow next door and slammed the door behind him.

* * *

Jonathan Harper parked his car in the Cozzi Cove lot, and heard a door slam toward the other end of the cove. After lifting his bags and getting out of his car, he walked along the cove while recalling his day at the Horror Convention. Actors playing ghosts, goblins, witches, warlocks, and werewolves had tried to engage him, but Jonathan's focus remained only on Vlad Lesti as Dracula. Every time Jonathan had tried to make eye contact with Vlad, the actor had looked away, staying in character as he twirled his cape, autographed customers' vampire kits, and hovered over delighted patron's necks while wearing his plastic fangs. Jonathan was so upset that he didn't even take the severed marshmallow head on a chocolate guillotine giveaway. Instead, he'd left the convention early and went grocery shopping.

He entered his bungalow, petted Renfield, and went through to the kitchen to put away his groceries. He then sat at the kitchen table staring into space.

Jonathan wasn't sure how much time had passed when Renfield whined for his dinner. He prepared a meal for Renfield and himself, and they ate at the table and on the bamboo floor respectively.

After cleaning up from dinner, Jonathan changed into a T-shirt and shorts and sat on his front porch, petting Renfield next to him and gazing out at the cove. Jonathan rocked back and forth, still reeling from Vlad's unexpected kiss.

As if illustrating his thoughts, the sky over the calm bay exploded in streaks of mahogany, marigold, and amethyst, and then turned gray. Jonathan heard a knock at the door and wished upon a bright star in the dark sky. His wish was granted as he opened the door to Vlad and Barnabas.

"Barnabas wanted to visit his pal." Vlad's face seemed to beg for affection.

Jonathan looked down at Renfield and Barnabas kissing. "I think they're more than pals."

Renfield and Barnabas scurried under the glider to cuddle.

Jonathan took in Vlad, looking terrific in an indigo dress shirt and black slacks. "I want to apologize."

"That should be my line." Vlad walked in. "You didn't do anything wrong."

"I didn't mean to push my beliefs on you. I'm sure it was just as annoying as someone with a religious tract or book at your door."

Vlad started laughing.

"What is it?"

Still laughing, Vlad said, "You know how I get rid of those people?"

Jonathan shook his head no.

"I tell them I'm gay, which is totally ironic, because throughout my whole life I've thought I was straight. Until last night."

"You mean when you kissed me?"

"Yeah."

"It was just a kiss. I mean, it was an incredible, very nice kiss."

"Easy for you to say. You're gay." Vlad sat on the rocking chair and rubbed his forehead.

Jonathan sat across from him. "Vlad, it was probably just all the vampire talk."

"Maybe I am descended from the man who inspired Stoker to write *Dracula*, and some of my personality traits stem from him. Who knows? To be honest, who cares? Last night, I wanted to kiss you. And I want to kiss you right now. And that's a huge problem."

"It's not a problem for me."

Vlad rose and paced the sun porch. "It's a problem for *me* because I've never been attracted to a guy before."

"Nobody's ever attracted to me. Are you sure you have this right?"

Vlad smiled at him. "I liked you from the first moment I met you on the cove. I thought it was just friendship. But there's more going on here."

"Maybe you're bisexual?"

"And I just realize this at fifty years old?"

"Maybe you're sexual orientation is fluid. Like Dracula's."

Vlad glared at him.

"I'm just trying to help."

Vlad sat on the rocking chair. "I know. None of this is your fault."

"Why is it anybody's fault? You said you're not homophobic."

"I'm not."

"Then you should know there's nothing wrong with being gay."

"Of course not—if you're gay. But something is very wrong with being gay if you're straight."

"Bram Stoker was married to a woman, like many gay men in the late nineteenth century. But he was in love with his business manager, Henry Irving. And it's common knowledge that *Dracula* has a homoerotic subtext with the coffin representing the closet, and Dracula's secret night life as a code for the existence of gay men in that time."

"But we're in *this* time. And two men can fall in love, get married, and raise a family in the light. Which is a good thing. For *gay* people."

Jonathan tried to be as delicate as possible. "Many people believe sexual orientation is genetic. Could it be possible that you also inherited the gay gene from your ancestors in Alba Iulia?"

"It would be an incredibly dormant gene, waiting this long to come out."

"Genetic science is still new. Maybe we all have genes and hormones that evolve with time."

Vlad rested his head in his hands. "I can't believe this is happening."

Jonathan placed a hand on his shoulder. "I'm sorry you're attracted to me. If I were you, I wouldn't be very happy about that either."

"No, Jonathan, I didn't mean it that way." Vlad gazed at him. "Have you eaten dinner yet?"

Jonathan nodded. "I made myself a hamburger, scalloped potatoes, and a salad. There's some left in the refrigerator. As rare as you like your meat, I can have dinner ready for you in a minute—literally.

"Perfect. Thank you."

A few minutes later, they were seated next to each other at the kitchen table with Vlad inhaling a very rare hamburger. Renfield and Barnabas sat under the table at their feet.

Vlad asked Jonathan between bites, "What would you do?"

"If I liked raw cow meat?"

"If you were attracted to a woman for the first time?"

"I find lots of women attractive, but I'm not attracted *to* them. I can't imagine I ever would be."

"I'm an actor, remember? Pretend for me."

"I would probably try dating her."

"You're just saying that because you're hot for me."

"Who said I'm hot for you?"

Vlad cocked his head at Jonathan.

"Okay, I find you very attractive."

"No kidding."

"If you're so straight, how do you know I'm attracted to you?"

"Straight guys know when a gay guy is hot for us."

Jonathan lifted his chin. "It's been my experience that some straight guys think all gay guys are attracted them."

"That's nuts." Vlad asked, "Do you have anything to drink?"

"Some leftover red wine from the other night."

"Great."

Jonathan served Vlad a glass of wine.

Vlad took a sip. "Are you trying to get me drunk and have your way with me?"

"Yes, I do that with all the sexually questioning vampires I entertain."

They shared a smile.

Vlad's shoulders relaxed. "Jonathan, I don't mean to dump all this on you."

"Dump what?" Jonathan asked, taking a seat again. "You met a very unattached man close to your age, and we hit it off, like our dogs."

"I met a man who thinks I'm descended from vampires."

"There's that. But there's also the fact that we enjoy each other's company. And that said man hasn't had a date in countless years. And he's getting quite long in the tooth, no pun intended. And as you've picked up, he likes you."

"You really think we should go out on a date?"

"Technically, this is our third date. Or fourth, if you include the night on the cove."

"Some date this is. All I've done is freak out about being attracted to you." Vlad finished his dinner. "Let's sit out on the porch."

Once they were seated on the glider with the dogs underneath them, Vlad asked, "What do two guys do on a date?"

"I don't think you're ready for that."

"I mean, what do you talk about?"

"The same thing a man and a woman talk about—our families, jobs, likes and dislikes."

"Where do gay guys go on a date?"

"Out to dinner or in to dinner, and then maybe to a movie, play, or out dancing."

"What do you talk about as the date winds down?"

"One guy tells the other why he's attracted to him."

Vlad laughed. "Is that a hint?"

Jonathan batted his eyelashes. "Is it my animal magnetism?"

Vlad seemed pensive. "I'm attracted to you because you're funny, smart, a good listener, entertaining, and quirky as all hell. You seem to understand me."

"Not exactly passion overflowing, but I'll take it."

Vlad took his hand. "Jonathan, this is all new for me, but I want to be honest with you. I think you're adorable and sweet and sexy. And I've never said that to another guy before."

Jonathan smiled. "There's something else two guys do on a date after dinner."

"What's that?"

"What we did last night."

Vlad returned the smile. "Do you want me to kiss you again?"

"How else will you know if your feelings are real, or just a passing thing?"

"You're right." Vlad placed his long fingers on the sides of Jonathan's face, and brought him closer for a long, wet, sensuous kiss. Jonathan wrapped his arms around Vlad and returned the kiss.

"Well?" Jonathan asked.

"That was amazing."

"Agreed."

"Are you disappointed that I didn't bite your neck?"

"We'll get there." Jonathan kissed him again. And then again.

Vlad hugged Jonathan and then rose. "It's late. I better go."

"Where?"

"Don't get excited, not to the cemetery. I need to head back to my bungalow to try to sort this out, and then get some sleep so I can work tomorrow at the convention. Thank you for dinner." Vlad and Barnabas walked to the front door.

Jonathan and Renfield followed them to the door. "Can I help?"

"You can go out on a real date with me tomorrow night. To Carla's Seafood Restaurant."

"I'd like that."

"Good. I'll pick you up after the convention."

Jonathan held his shoulder. "Vlad, whatever you're thinking or going through, I'm incredibly flattered that you like me. And I think you're well worth the wait."

Vlad kissed Jonathan's cheek. "Good night."

After they left, Jonathan sat on the rocking chair, and Renfield placed his paw on Jonathan's knee. Petting Renfield's paw, Jonathan said, "Can you believe it? After all these years, I'm falling in love with someone, Renfield. And though he doesn't know it yet, I think Vlad's falling in love with me too." Renfield rested his head on Jonathan's lap, and Jonathan stroked his fur. "And the man I love is a descendent of Count Dracula!" Jonathan laughed merrily.

* * *

As he headed down the cove, Billy Dean smiled at Jonathan Harper laughing on the porch of Bungalow Three. It was nice to see people having a good time at Cozzi Cove. Billy Dean had eaten ham hocks and eggs for breakfast, cleaned the bungalows, had lunch with Jesus and John in their bungalow, worked out at the college gym, finished turndown service, and attended rehearsal for his school play.

He knocked on the door of Bungalow Seven, and Jesus and John gave him a warm hug and invited him back to the patio. They sat at the white oak table, and Jesus spooned ratatouille onto Billy Dean's plate as John loaded it with vegetable kabobs, hummus, bulgur and asparagus salad, and grilled tofu.

"Y'all are spoiling me," Billy Dean said, loving every minute of it. "I may never go home."

"We love having you here," John said.

"And I love being here." Billy Dean ate the delicious food heartily. "I never thought I could live without eating meat, but y'all have changed my way of thinking."

"We've changed your way of thinking about a lot of things," Jesus said with a smile.

"My grampa would never believe I'd eat dinner without seconds of beef and pork," Billy Dean said.

"Our ancestors made their decisions, now it's time for us to make ours," Jesus said.

Billy Dean said between bites, "Are y'all close to your folks?"

"We're all close to our parents, whether we care to admit it or not," Jesus said.

"Jesus and I believe that before we are born we each pick our parents," John added.

Billy Dean pondered that. "How do we know who to choose?"

"We select people who have something to teach us," Jesus said. "So we can learn enough to get to the next level of consciousness."

"I guess my folks have taught me some things," Billy Dean said. "How about y'all?"

"My parents argue constantly. They taught me that I don't want a marriage like that," John replied.

"Mine criticize and judge just about everything I do. That taught me not to be judgmental," Jesus added.

"It isn't just what our parents overtly teach us that's important," John said. "It's what we learn by watching them and breaking the pattern of dysfunction."

"Mama and Daddy are busy with my younger brother and sisters," Billy Dean said. "They don't pay me much mind."

"Maybe what you can learn from them is that you want to be with people who notice you more often," Jesus said. "Enjoy your company. Value your gifts."

"My gifts?" Billy Dean asked.

"Your beauty, strength, courage, and compassion for others," Jesus replied.

"And your sound work ethic and honesty," John replied.

"I have all those gifts?" Billy Dean couldn't believe his ears.

"Those and probably more," Jesus answered.

"I wish I was half as together as you are when I was your age," John said.

Billy Dean rested a hand on each of their shoulders. "I don't know what y'all were like in college, but right now, you're pretty terrific."

After dinner the three men headed for the front bedroom. Billy Dean enjoyed another night of lovemaking with Jesus and John that somehow was even more earthshattering than the night before.

Afterward, they lay naked together with Billy Dean in the middle, and he rested his head on Jesus's chest as John curled his arm around Billy Dean's waist. Unable to sleep, Billy Dean asked, "Do y'all do yoga and meditate?"

"When we wake up in the morning and in the late afternoons," Jesus answered.

"Does it relax you?"

"Would you like us to teach you?" John asked.

Billy Dean nodded.

Jesus rose from the bed and demonstrated the downward dog, warrior, ragdoll, and tree poses. "The poses massage the organs, channel breath and energy throughout the body, and bring you closer to nirvana."

"Nirvana?" Billy Dean asked.

"All knowledge and energy," John said. "It's the perfect place that lies within each of us."

John stood up and did the poses with Jesus. Billy Dean also got up and tried the poses, but he couldn't do any of them. "I'm not limber enough."

Jesus smiled. "Maybe we should start with meditation." Jesus sat on the bed with his back straight, his legs entwined, and his forefingers touching his thumbs. John did the same. Billy Dean tried but his legs wouldn't cooperate. Jesus said, "You can meditate seated comfortably."

Billy Dean sat with his back resting against the headboard.

Jesus led John and Billy Dean through a rhythmic breathing meditation, a visualization in a garden, and finally a Hindu mantra meditation.

Some time later, Billy Dean woke up in bed cuddled between Jesus and John. Billy Dean didn't know how long they'd been asleep as he listened to Jesus breathing heavily. Then Jesus's breathing turned into moaning. Billy Dean opened his eyes and noticed Jesus was soaking wet. Suddenly, Jesus let out a piercing scream. Billy Dean and John shot up. Jesus now leaned on one elbow sobbing.

John quickly moved to Jesus's other side, and Jesus collapsed into his arms.

Not knowing what else to do, Billy Dean rubbed Jesus's back. Like his grampa did when Billy Dean had a nightmare, Billy Dean whispered in Jesus's ear, "It's just a bad dream, boy. And dreams, unlike us, quickly go away when we're awake." Jesus took Billy Dean's hand and squeezed it hard.

John pulled Jesus up so he could sit back against the headboard. He ran his hand through Jesus's hair as he kissed his forehead, soothing him, and then rested against the headboard with his arm around Jesus. Billy Dean sat on Jesus's other side, still holding his hand.

After resting like that for a while, Jesus calmed down, and his breathing returned to normal. He turned to John, "You'd better explain."

John kissed Jesus's cheek and then turned toward Billy Dean. "A little over a year ago, Jesus and I were in our loincloths and angel wings at a funeral with the Angels. A gay man had died. His husband, daughter, and parents were walking from their car into an open and affirming church. An evangelical group of protesters held their signs and shouted their hateful rhetoric as usual about Adam and Eve. The Angels formed a line around the church, spread out our wings, and sang 'Amazing Grace' to drown out the protestors. We had our backs to the hatemongers, and one of them ran toward us, lifted his sign, and lowered it over me. Jesus saw him before I did and pushed me out of the way. When Jesus lifted his hands to push the man away, the wooden sign came crashing down on his hands. The man raised the sign again and hit Jesus on his head and once more on his back. All the while, the man shouted out words of hate. Jesus was in incredible pain, and he finally lost consciousness. I stayed by his side while one of the Angels called for an ambulance and another phoned the police. The rest of them held down the attacker."

"Did he go to prison?" Billy Dean asked.

John sighed. "He got probation only. For one month."

"But that was a hate crime!" Billy Dean said.

"We got an evangelical judge appointed by a Republican governor," John replied.

"I still have nightmares where it's happening all over again," Jesus said. He wiped the tears off his cheeks with his still shaking forearm.

"What about the Reiki, meditation, and yoga?" Billy Dean asked. "Don't they help?"

Jesus smiled weakly. "Just like your love for your savior, sometimes it isn't enough."

Billy Dean was saddened that such a sweet, warm, and loving person had that burden to bear. And that John had had to help Jesus through it alone. Billy Dean leaned over and kissed the scars on Jesus's head, back, and hands.

Jesus and John wrapped their arms around Billy Dean, and the three of them cuddled together against the dark night.

* * *

At the other end of the cove, Cal was lying in bed in his boxers when Michael got home from Tommy's bar.

Michael quickly sat at the desk, turned on his laptop, and began working.

"Don't I get a 'hello'?"

"Malcolm texted me."

"How did he get your phone number?"

"Malcolm's a journalist. He can find out anything."

"What did his text say?"

"He really liked my revised article. And he asked me to e-mail him my resume, some sample articles from school, and a statement of my photojournalistic philosophy."

"What's your photojournalistic philosophy?"

"I haven't decided yet. Now let me concentrate."

Cal got out of bed and kissed Michael's neck. "I know you're excited. And I understand this is a terrific opportunity with Malcolm. But I want you to know I don't trust the guy. And I'm skeptical about his sincerity."

Michael looked up at Cal with hurt in his eyes. "Because how could any editor ever think I'm talented? There has to be an ulterior motive that has to do with Malcolm getting back at you. Because everyone knows you're the one anyone would want, not me."

"I didn't say that."

"Your sister said it for you."

Cal sat at the edge of the bed. "Michael, the guy is living on the down-low. That speaks to his lack of honesty and character. He revels in journalism that excludes people like us. And he clearly likes younger guys, and always has."

Michael spun around in his chair. "Cal, one of the biggest magazine editors in the country is interested in my work. He wants to be my mentor and may offer me a job. I won't let you or Taylor ruin this for me." He turned his back to Cal and went back to work.

Cal shook his head and climbed back into bed. He rested against the headboard and picked up his great-grandfather's diary to read the next entry.

July 15, 1937.

I apologize for not writing in a while. I had an accident last month while building Cozzi Cove. A metal beam propped up against the foundation fell on my leg. It hurt like the dickens. My assistant removed the beam and drove me to Doc Robinson's. The doc said I needed to stay off it for two weeks. Later, I got a bad fever. Doc Robinson came over and gave me some pills. I felt delirious and weak. While Mama took care of me, my assistant worked at Cozzi Cove by himself so we wouldn't get behind in our schedule. He also visited me every night. Once my fever went down, he brought me dinner from Mangione's. I put the baby in with Mama, and my assistant and I talked until the wee hours of the night about everything that had happened at the site. When I thanked him for being such a good friend, he sat at the edge of my bed and rested his hand on the side of my face. He said he was really worried about me when I was sick, and he did not know what he would do if he ever lost me. I could not resist pressing my lips against his. I thought he might sock me in the jaw, but instead, he placed his arms around me and hugged my neck. We lay back in my bed and took off our boots and clothes. Entwined in each other's bodies, I told him I felt reborn. We hugged, kissed, and caressed. I was surprised when I heard myself tell him I loved him. And I was even more surprised when he replied that he loved me too. With our tools hard as rocks, we used our hands to bring each other to blissful release. We rested in each other's arms, never wanting to separate. Now I know how people feel when they're in love. And it is the best feeling in the world.

Cal fell asleep with a smile on his face to the sound of Michael clicking away on his laptop, glad his great-grandfather had found true love.

CHAPTER EIGHT

The next morning, Billy Dean woke gloriously in Jesus and John's arms. While he showered, Jesus and John made breakfast and set the kitchen table. After he got dressed, Billy Dean joined them at the kitchen table for spinach and sundried tomato omelets, blueberry oatmeal waffles with raw honey, vegetarian bacon, eight-grain toast, and three-greens smoothies.

"After breakfast back home, I always felt bloated. Your meals are delicious and leave me as energetic as a high school kid in the hay loft on prom night."

As they enjoyed the early morning feast, Jesus said, "I'm sorry about last night."

John squeezed Jesus's hand.

Billy Dean squeezed Jesus's other hand. "I'm sorry that happened to you. If I was with y'all in front of that church, I'd have taken care of that guy for you," Billy Dean said.

Jesus kissed the top of Billy Dean's head.

"Does he still live around here?" Billy Dean asked.

Jesus nodded. "I saw him in town yesterday when I was shopping at the grocery store. I assume that's why I had the dream last night."

"He's free to walk around town?"

"Free as a bird," John said.

Rage rose inside Billy Dean. "If I had been with you at that store, I'd have told him to give his heart to Jesus 'cause his ass is mine."

"I don't have to tell you that Jesus turned the other cheek and forgave those who hurt him, even on the cross," John said to Billy Dean.

"So you've forgiven this guy for beating Jesus so badly?" Billy Dean asked in shock.

"He has his own demons. John and I forgiving him is about us, not about him."

"I met a lot of people back home who called themselves 'religious,' but they gossiped and gloated. Y'all are the real deal."

Jesus kissed Billy Dean on the cheek. John kissed him on the other cheek.

"What's that for?" Billy Dean asked.

"We like having you here," Jesus said.

John confirmed this by playfully mussing Billy Dean's thick blond hair.

"And I like being here." Billy Dean helped himself to more vegetarian bacon and another omelet. "But I have to leave soon to clean the bungalows. As Grampa would say, 'Cal keeps me busier than a moth in an old mitten.'"

"How about joining us at the main beach this afternoon?" Jesus asked.

"Looks like you could use a break," John added.

Billy Dean had moved to the Jersey Shore and hadn't yet spent any time at the ocean. "I'd like that." He finished his breakfast and rose. "See y'all when I'm through with my cleaning."

"Come over for lunch. Then we'll head to the beach," John said.

Billy Dean hugged Jesus and John and then flew out the front door of Bungalow Seven. As he raced down the cove, he nearly bumped into Andrew Urban, coming out of Bungalow Six.

* * *

Andrew had spent the night and most of the morning in tears. Having lost Nijad, Andrew had put on a turquoise swimsuit, grabbed a beach towel, and headed for his car alone. After a short drive, he parked at the main beach, and walked on the warm white sand to a spot near a sand dune. He unfolded his towel and sat on it. Then, as he stared at the sky as blue as his feelings, a seagull flew overhead and landed on the jagged rocks. As the white foamy waves pounded against the rocks, Andrew turned his head to watch the seagull fly off. He saw Nijad sitting on a beach towel about ten feet away. Nijad looked away. Andrew did too. They looked at each other again. Then they each looked away again.

Feeling as if he would burst if he didn't speak to Nijad, Andrew walked over to him. "I knocked on your bungalow door yesterday, and again this morning."

"I know."

"Please let me try to explain."

Nijad looked up at him, squinting his dark eyes against the sun. "What's there to explain? Knowing I'm bisexual, you played dress up to mock me."

"No, Nijad, that's not what I did."

"I was there, remember?" Nijad opened a book and began reading.

"Nijad, please listen to me."

Nijad kept reading. Just as Andrew was about to give up and go back to his beach towel, Nijad said, "Did you put on sunscreen?"

Andrew shook his head and his blond hair swept around his face. "I forgot it."

"Use this." Nijad reached into his beach bag and tossed Andrew a bottle of lotion. Andrew applied the lotion and asked, "Can you put some on my back?"

Nijad took the bottle and rubbed some lotion onto Andrew's square-shaped back. "You're too fair to go out without this."

When Nijad had finished, Andrew said, "Thank you. Can I put some on your back?"

Nijad nodded, and Andrew rubbed the creamy coconut-scented lotion into the dark ripples of muscle on Nijad's broad, V-shaped back.

"Can I sit with you?" Andrew asked.

Nijad pointed to an empty spot on his beach towel.

When Andrew was seated, he looked into Nijad's handsome face. "I want to apologize."

"For what? You had your fun."

"No, I didn't. What I did was terribly wrong. I know that. But I really like you. And I think I'm falling in love with you."

"You have an odd way of showing it."

"I know. That's the point. In the past when I liked someone, I hid Annabel away. Once a guy I liked met her, he'd take off. I thought if you could get to know and like Annabel before I told you the truth, perhaps you wouldn't leave when I finally fessed up. What I did was incredibly selfish. And I understand how you'd want nothing more to do with me. I can't say that I blame you." Tears streamed down Andrew's cheeks.

Nijad leaned back on his hands, and his shoulders rose like mountains. "Are you still playing with me?"

"I wish I were. But it's not what you're thinking."

"I don't understand."

"Does it matter now?"

"Yes, it does. Please, start at the beginning. What's been going on?"

After taking a deep breath, Andrew said, "As I mentioned, when I was a kid my mother had severe mood swings. She was the most loving and sweet mom a kid could have one moment, and then the next, she'd chase me around the house calling me names. Those were the good days. On the bad days if I didn't run and hide fast enough, she'd beat me with her wooden spoon until I bled, and then she beat me some more."

"That's awful. I'm sorry about that...for you."

"I'm not telling you about this for pity. I want you to understand."

"But I still don't. Understand what?"

"About dissociative identity disorder."

Nijad looked at him with curiosity, confusion, and compassion.

"I was afraid and lonely as a child, so in my head I created an alter, another personality to keep me company, calm me down, commiserate with me, and even protect me."

"And that is Annabel?"

"Yes. I read a book about England, and I was fascinated with their culture. So I invented Annabel, a little British girl who was strong, resilient, resourceful, and always on my side. At first, Annabel was just a thought in my head, a make-believe playmate. Then, she became a part of me. Finally, she was my twin sister."

Nijad seemed to be putting the pieces together in his mind. "So when Annabel said your mother beat her for wearing makeup, your mother really beat *you*? And when Annabel said she protected you from your mother, she meant *you* became Annabel and found the courage to hide, run away, or stand up to your mother?"

Andrew nodded.

Nijad rested his elbows on his knees. "Wasn't it a problem when Annabel appeared at school?"

"At first Annabel only came out at home."

"And then?"

"As I got older, she'd go out to clubs, dances, and parties. When other people saw Annabel and questioned me about it, I made up the story about Annabel being my twin sister."

"But you said Annabel went off to college and lived for years in Kent?"

"I was seeing a psychiatrist. And Annabel came out much less frequently. When she did, I told people my sister was visiting from England."

"What changed recently?"

"I was gay bashed coming out of a bar one night. The guy beat me up pretty badly. I recovered—physically."

"And all the fears came back about your mother?"

"And so did Annabel."

"That's why you told me Annabel moved back in with you?"

"Yes. And I was so pleased when you liked Annabel."

"I liked her very much." Nijad rubbed his forehead. "But I would have liked knowing the truth even more."

Tears stained Andrew's eyes. "I know not telling you was unfair. And for that I am so very sorry."

Nijad looked out at the ocean.

"Well, that's what I wanted to say. And that I think you're a wonderful person. And under other circumstances, I would have been honored to date you. I hope you find someone nice and truthful, with none of my problems. You deserve that." With tears still flowing down his cheeks, Andrew rose and walked back to his towel. He sat and buried his head in his hands. After a good long cry, Andrew realized he would always be alone. It was absurd to think that anyone would want to get involved with someone like him, especially a man as perfect as Nijad.

It was time to leave. Andrew got up from his towel and turned to find Nijad approaching him. Nijad handed him a starfish with a pink center and legs of vermillion and indigo.

"I found this on the beach."

Andrew did a double take. "It's beautiful."

"Like you. And like Annabel." Nijad leaned in and kissed the tears on Andrew's cheeks.

"Does this mean you forgive me?"

"You're the victim, not the perpetrator. I was a fool not to see that."

Nijad offered his hand. Andrew rested the starfish on the towel, took Nijad's hand, and they walked along the water's edge.

After walking for a while in silence, Nijad asked, "How will this work?"

"Work?"

"Our relationship."

Andrew's heart almost leapt out of his chest. "You want to continue seeing me?"

Nijad squeezed his hand. "I...neither of us can promise this will work, but I'd like to give it a try, if you do too."

Unable to contain himself, Andrew threw himself into Nijad's strong arms, and they kissed. "I feel like Mack with Brady in *Teen Beach*."

They shared a laugh.

Andrew rattled on, "We don't live very far from each other. I get plenty of days off. I can drive to visit you, and you can do the same with me. And even when I'm working, we can e-mail, phone, and text each other."

A crease formed on Nijad's smooth forehead. "I meant how does it work with Andrew and Annabel."

"Well, you and Annabel like each other. That's a good start."

"Do you decide when Annabel...takes over?"

"Sometimes. Other times it just happens." Andrew smiled. "As you saw, Annabel has a strong will."

"Do you always dress as Annabel when she...comes out?"

"Not always, but a lot of the time."

"How will I know if I'm with you or Annabel?"

"You'll know."

Nijad smiled. "I guess I will."

A wave broke close to the shore and showered their lower legs with cool white foam. Andrew said, "Sometimes Annabel stays away for quite a while. Other times, she's relentless as she was this week."

"Why was that?"

"Because she wanted to spend time with you."

Nijad rubbed his strong chin. "You believe Annabel came out because of me?"

"Sometimes Annabel comes out when I feel stressed, lonely, or afraid. Other times, like this week, it just feels right for Annabel to take over at times."

"When Annabel is in control, do you know what she says and does?"

"I didn't always when I was a kid, but now I do."

They passed a little boy and girl playing in the sand, and then stopped walking.

"Can you let Annabel out now?" Nijad asked.

"Is that what you want?" Andrew asked.

Nijad nodded.

Annabel placed her hand on her hip. "You left me mid-bloody kiss!"

"I didn't understand about you and Andrew."

Annabel smiled. "And do you *now*?"

"Not really, but I'm trying."

"Smashing." Annabel kissed Nijad on the cheek, and they continued walking. "Did you miss me?"

"Andrew kept me company."

"He's good at that. But just between us, Andrew can be a bit of a bore at times."

Nijad laughed. "Careful. Andrew can hear you."

"Cheeky bugger, aren't you?"

"You'll have to get to know me better to find out."

"I'm game."

"Good."

Annabel joyously ran into the water.

Nijad called out, "What are you doing?"

"Swimming. It's an ocean. Come with me!"

Annabel swam out into the deep water, and Nijad followed. They swam through the waves and then over them. When they reached shallow water, Annabel splashed Nijad, and he splashed back. Laughing like teenagers, Annabel tried to dunk Nijad under the water, but Nijad stood firm like a tree trunk.

Annabel wrapped her arms and legs around Nijad's powerful body. Then she rested her head on his mountainous chest. "I really like you."

"I really like you too."

"Are you okay with the brother and sister thing?"

"I'm still sorting through it in my head."

"Does this help?" Annabel kissed Nijad on the lips.

Nijad kissed her back. "It could have its benefits."

Annabel laughed. They swam some more and then returned back to the sand dune. After plopping down on Nijad's towel, Annabel said, "I'm ravenous. Andrew didn't make breakfast."

Nijad opened his beach bag. "Care to share a turkey, Monterey Jack cheese, lettuce, and tomato sandwich on pumpernickel bread?"

"Lovely!"

As they ate, Annabel lifted her blue eyes to the blue sky. "Delicious!"

Nijad also shared his bottled water.

"You're a true gentleman."

"My pleasure."

When they had finished, Nijad asked, "May I speak with Andrew now?"

"Growing tired of me?"

Nijad laughed. "No. I need to ask Andrew something."

A sober look, and Andrew had returned. He touched Nijad's knee. "Did you enjoy your time with Annabel?"

"Yes, I did." Nijad took his hand. "I want to be honest with you."

"Unlike I was with you." Andrew looked down at the sand.

"Please, stop beating yourself up. I need to explain something. The reason I was upset when you didn't tell me the truth about Annabel was that I'm falling in love with you. And I don't want there to be any secrets between us."

Andrew couldn't believe his ears. "There won't be. Ever again!" He slid his arms around Nijad and rested his head on his wide shoulder.

"Whatever's going on with Annabel, and with Andrew, if we have any hope of making this work, you'll need to be honest with me."

"I will. I promise."

"Come to my bungalow for dinner tonight?" Nijad asked.

"I'd like that."

"Will Annabel come too?"

"We'll see." They shared another kiss. "And come to *my* bungalow for dinner tomorrow night?"

Nijad seemed to blink back a tear.

"What's wrong?" Andrew asked.

"That's our last night at Cozzi Cove."

"We'll have to come back again sometime."

"I like the sound of that."

After another kiss, Andrew held the starfish to his heart. "Me too."

* * *

On the other side of the dune, Billy Dean sat on a large turquoise beach blanket between Jesus and John. Jesus rubbed suntan lotion on John's back, John worked on Billy Dean's back, and Billy Dean applied the lotion to Jesus's back.

Looking out at the white rippled water crashing against the jagged rocks, Billy Dean said, "I'm dryer than a tree bribing a dog."

Jesus smiled. "I love your grampa's expressions."

John opened the cooler and passed out coconut mango juices. Billy Dean took a sip and let the coolness wash down inside him as he watched a white seagull soar through the royal-blue sky.

"Billy Dean," Jesus said.

Unaware of how much time had gone by, Billy Dean opened his eyes. "Did I conk out?"

"Just for a few minutes," John said.

"When were you diagnosed with narcolepsy?" Jesus asked.

"When I was in the third grade," Billy Dean replied, recalling that Jesus was a nurse. "I remember my teacher Miss Hocum pitching a hissy fit in class when I kept nodding off. She called in my mama and recommended that Mama take me to Dr. Teter. Doc didn't know what was wrong with me, so he sent me to another doctor in Birmingham. Dr. Kiley glued these wires to my head and ran some tests. After that he told my mama what I had."

"Were you frightened?" John asked.

"Not really. I fell asleep in his office," Billy Dean replied.

"Is it safe for you to swim in the ocean?" Jesus asked.

Billy Dean nodded. "The cool ocean water helps keep me awake."

"Then let's keep you awake." John ran into the water, his aqua Speedo bright against the waves.

Jesus followed in his gold Speedo, and Billy Dean was last wearing kelly-green trunks. The three of them swam out to the deeper water and splashed each other between fits of laughter. When a large wave came their way, they rode it back into the shallower water.

"Let's make a sandcastle," Billy Dean said.

Jesus and John followed Billy Dean to the water's edge, where Billy Dean clumped together wet sand with dry and began his creation.

Kneeling next to him, Jesus said, "That doesn't look like a sandcastle."

"It's not a sandcastle like in the days of kings, queens, and knights. It's my castle. The home I'd like to have someday."

"Tell us about it," John said.

"This here's the wraparound porch for sitting out at night and drinking lemonade." Billy Dean explained as he worked. "The living room is next with a big fireplace for roasting marshmallows. Back here is the kitchen to make lots of food. As you know, I have a big appetite. And right here is the dining room to eat it. Up the stairs is a bedroom with a balcony overlooking an ocean like this one. I'll make it big enough for the three of us."

Obviously overwhelmed, Jesus and John kissed Billy Dean right in front of the other people on the beach. "Would you like that, Billy Dean?" Jesus asked.

Billy Dean replied, "I'd like that more than a mosquito likes a hole in a screen door."

The three of them laughed, and then Jesus and John kissed him again.

Billy Dean continued working on his creation. "I don't mean to be nosier than a cat at a tuna factory, but are y'all married?"

"We don't need a legal contract to prove our love," Jesus said, taking John's hand.

"But what if one of y'all gets sick and has to take care of the other one?" Billy Dean asked.

John created a sand bridge over a pond in front of Billy Dean's house. "We'll cross that bridge when the time comes."

A little blond boy approached them. "Can I play with your house?"

Billy Dean smiled. "It's all yours, sugar."

As the three men walked back to their blanket, Billy Dean asked, "Y'all ever think about having kids?"

Jesus sat down on the blanket. "We've talked about it, but it hasn't felt right."

John joined him. "I work with kids all day at the center. I feel as if I have lots of children."

"I helped raised my younger brothers and sisters." Billy Dean joined them on the blanket. "So I know what y'all mean."

Jesus looked at John and Billy Dean. "We may have kids someday. When the time is right."

Billy Dean looked at his watch. "I best be getting back to Cozzi Cove. I promised Cal I'd clean out the supply shed."

"We'll drive you," Jesus said.

"There's something we want to show you first," John said.

They packed their things and headed to John's car. Once inside, John drove in the opposite direction of Cozzi Cove.

"Where are we going?" Billy Dean asked.

"We're showing you our house," Jesus said.

Ten minutes later, they got out of the car, and Billy Dean's jaw dropped at the sight of Jesus and John's house. "It's just like the sand house on the beach. It even has John's bridge over the pond in front!

"Come inside." Jesus led them across the wraparound porch and into the living room.

"The big fireplace!" Billy Dean said.

John walked them through the dining room and into the kitchen. "And a kitchen large enough to feed your appetite."

Jesus led them upstairs to look at the bedrooms, and Billy Dean stood out on the balcony of the master bedroom and looked at the ocean in the distance. "I would feel like a king on this."

Jesus and John smiled at each other. After viewing the second bedroom and study, they went back downstairs.

Billy Dean whistled as he gazed at the homey curtains, rugs, and paintings. "This place is prettier than a mound of butter on wheat cakes. And the walls are my favorite color, sky blue."

"I'm glad you like it, Billy Dean," Jesus said. "Care to join us for dinner tonight?"

"Here, or at Cozzi Cove?"

"Neither. At Carla's Seafood Restaurant." John said.

"It'll have to be a late supper again since I have play rehearsal," Billy Dean said.

"Fine with us," John said.

"Come to our bungalow when you get back," Jesus said.

"I will."

As they drove back to Cozzi Cove in silence, Billy Dean counted his blessings for having met Jesus and John at the cove. He knew that Jesus approved. Both of them.

Exiting the car at the Cozzi Cove parking lot, Billy Dean could hear voices coming from the backyard of the main bungalow.

* * *

Michael and Cal were having lunch on the patio of the main bungalow. That is, Cal was eating lunch. Michael, in his white T-shirt and black work chinos, was sitting at the white oak table on a sea blue cushioned white wicker chair staring at his cell phone, willing Malcolm to call.

When Michael looked up, Cal asked, "Don't you like the salade Niçoise?"

Michael glanced at the bowl in front of him brimming with baby greens, cherry tomatoes, string beans, dark tuna, hardboiled egg wedges, and anchovies covered in raspberry vinaigrette.

"It looks great." He took a bite while gazing at his phone.

"Ever hear the expression 'a watched pot doesn't boil'?"

"It sounds like something Billy Dean's grampa would say."

Cal took his hand. "Michael, you're a talented photographer. Have faith in that. If Malcolm doesn't offer you a job, something else will come up."

Michael wasn't so easily convinced.

"I'm going to kill her!" Carla waddled onto the patio and lowered herself into one of the empty chairs at the table.

"Who are you going to kill?" Cal asked, serving her some of the salad.

"As if you don't know." Carla smelled the salad. "Tuna and anchovies? Really?"

"You were craving anchovies," Cal replied.

"That was last week. This week it's mussels."

Cal flexed his bicep. "Enjoy."

Carla swatted his arm away as if it were a fly. "No Cozzi will ever make me laugh again."

"You're a Cozzi now too, Carla."

Carla glared at Cal. "Don't remind me."

Digging back into his salad, Cal asked, "What did my sister do now?"

"A plethora of things, the latest being accepting the job offer in Paris."

Cal's jaw dropped. He retrieved an anchovy from the table, popped it back into his mouth, and swallowed. "What's wrong with that woman?"

"Too many things to mention in mixed company." Carla looked over at Michael. "How come you're so quiet?"

Michael continued staring at his phone. "I'm waiting for a job offer from Malcolm."

"Didn't anyone ever tell you a watched pot doesn't boil?" Carla said.

"Old people." Michael shrugged and ate more of his salad.

"What are you going to do about Taylor?" Cal asked Carla.

"I guess shooting her isn't a good option, since I wouldn't like prison food," Carla replied.

"You might like the prison matron," Michael said with a giggle.

"You won't be making jokes when Taylor gets back here, and I'm on the most wanted list," Carla said before stuffing an egg wedge into her mouth.

"When does the Parisian arrive?" Cal asked.

"Tomorrow," Carla replied with a sneer.

"What are you going to tell her?" Cal poured her some lemonade.

"That we're not under any circumstances moving to Paris." Carla drank some lemonade. "And if she wants this job, she can move there without me."

"Long distance relationships don't work," Michael said.

Carla did a double take. "How would *you* know?"

"A guy in one of my college classes was in one with a man from Switzerland," Michael explained.

"What happened?" Cal asked.

"His boyfriend ran off with a Swiss guard," Michael answered.

"Would you ever leave me for a Swiss guard?" Cal asked.

Michael kissed his nose. "Never. Only a royal guard in London. Those guys are hot."

Cal laughed. "Maybe I'll buy one of those tall hats and wear it to bed tonight."

"Blimey, baby."

Michael and Cal kissed.

Carla groaned. "Will you two get a room?"

"We have an entire resort," Cal said.

"Exactly!" Carla ate more of her salad before adding, "Michael, you're lucky you picked a Cozzi who has the sense not to leave his roots."

"Right, *his* roots," Michael said.

"That reminds me." Cal's face lit up like a jack-o'-lantern. "I read some more of my great-grandfather's diary, and great-granddad had a steamy affair with his young assistant carpenter. It seems like the two men were really in love."

"Ouch!" Carla exclaimed, holding her stomach. "The baby thinks he's a football kicker."

Cal smiled. "He must be happy his great-great grandfather was gay."

"Do you think the baby's gay?" Michael asked.

"It's pretty likely, given that his fathers and surrogate are gay," Cal replied. "Not to mention his great-grandfather."

"What did the sonogram show?" Michael asked.

"They only show gender, not sexual orientation," Carla said. "He may be straight. The three of us were brought up by straight parents, and we're not straight. Plus, we don't know the sexual orientation of the egg donor."

Michael hoped the baby was healthy, whatever his sexual orientation. He also hoped Malcolm would call with a job offer. He finished his salad, kissed Cal and Carla on the cheek, and left for work.

Michael jumped into his sports car and drove to Tommy Malone's bar in town. After parking in front of the bar, he headed inside, turned on the lights, and went about his usual routine of getting ready for customers.

The hours went by like months as Michael went through the motions of welcoming guests, serving drinks, and cleaning up, all the while wondering whether or not Malcolm would hire him.

As if by magic, the editor suddenly materialized in front of Michael's eyes, wearing a tan silk shirt, open at the neck, tight brown slacks, and designer beige loafers. His gold watch, rings, and neck chain glistened in the bar lighting.

Malcolm looked around the bar. "I like the netting, boat models, and nautical pictures. The sand on the floor is a bit much, though."

Michael banged his knee into the sink behind the bar. "Malcolm! Come in. Please, have a seat."

Malcolm sat at the bar across from Michael.

"What can I get for you?"

"A dark beer would be great."

"Coming right up." Michael's hands shook as he poured and served the beer, spilling white foam onto the bar.

"How much do I owe you?"

"It's on the house."

"Thanks."

"My pleasure."

They smiled at each other.

Michael deliberated on how to bring up the job possibility and came up with, "Did you get the materials I e-mailed to you?"

"I sure did. And I forwarded them to some of my managers." Malcolm took a sip of his beer.

"Any feedback yet?" Michael hoped that didn't sound too forward.

"Yes. As a matter of fact, young man, I come bearing good news."

"Good news?" Michael croaked out through a suddenly dry throat.

Malcolm nodded. "Our LA office is in need of a photojournalist to cover the comings and goings of people in the entertainment industry. Of course there are more applicants than unemployed actors in

Hollywood, but the manager of that office and I had a long talk. And we agree you're the man for the job."

Feeling faint, Michael sat down on a stool behind the bar. "You mean you want *me*?"

Malcolm placed his hand over Michael's. "I want you very much, Michael."

"I can't believe it. The job sounds perfect!"

"It is."

Then reality hit. "But it's in LA."

Malcolm nodded. "The home of the rich and famous."

"Cal won't leave Cozzi Cove. It's been in his family for generations."

Lines sprouted on Malcolm's forehead. "Doesn't Cal want you to be successful?"

"Of course he does."

Malcolm leaned on the bar and his biceps nearly burst out of his shirt. "Then why would he stand in the way of your success?"

"He wouldn't. But LA is six hours away by plane. A job like that requires availability day and night. When would Cal and I see each other? And we have a baby coming."

"What's more important to you, Michael? Having a career in photojournalism, or tending bar to be near your husband and baby?"

"I want a career."

"Good answer."

"But I also want a family."

"I have a family. But I'd never have become a senior editor if I didn't travel."

"Is there a possibility that something will open up in New York City?"

"I doubt it." Malcolm sat back on his stool. "I'm offering you the chance of a lifetime. A job most guys with a heck of a lot more experience than you would kill for. Are you really going to turn it down to vegetate in this little beach town?"

Taking a different angle, Michael asked, "How would I work with you as my mentor?"

"I fly to LA all the time for meetings. I have a penthouse apartment overlooking the mountains."

"Can I think about it?"

"Think fast. I can't promise the position will stay open for long." Malcolm swallowed the rest of his beer. "Stop by my bungalow tomorrow morning with your decision."

"All right."

"Think very carefully, Michael. An amazing opportunity like this will never come your way again." Malcolm left the bar.

Michael rested his head in his hands and thought about Cal and their soon-to-arrive baby.

CHAPTER NINE

That evening, Jonathan Harper parked at the lot at Cozzi Cove and walked to his bungalow. He had barely gotten through the day at the Horror Convention. The occult enthusiast hardly noticed the sword swallower, Frankenstein monster, or the witch flying on an electronic broomstick. Gazing at Vlad in his Dracula outfit as he flashed his giant fangs, Jonathan nearly burst from excitement over their upcoming date.

Shivers raced up and down Jonathan's spine as he opened the door of his bungalow, petted and fed Renfield, and then went into the front bedroom to change into a cherry-red dress shirt, gray slacks, and gray blazer. He combed the few hairs left on his head, while Renfield shined Jonathan's shoes with his fur. Hearing a knock at the front door, Jonathan hurried to the front porch with Renfield at his side.

With his heart pounding in his narrow chest, Jonathan opened the front door to Vlad, looking incredibly sexy in a white shirt, violet vest, and black slacks. His jet-black hair was gelled and slicked back behind his ears, making his strong, chiseled features seem even more vibrant.

"You look wonderful," Jonathan said, meaning it.

Vlad revealed his large white teeth. "So do you."

Barnabas raced over to Renfield. After sharing some kisses, they disappeared into the kitchen.

"I'm really glad we're going out to dinner," Jonathan said.

Vlad gestured to his car. "Shall we?"

After they entered the restaurant, Dotty seated them at a dimly lit corner table next to an anchor. They ordered Surf and Turf, but Vlad ate both steaks—blood rare—and Jonathan ate both lobsters.

Moving on to the potatoes au gratin and vegetable medley—minus the garlic, Vlad asked, "Tell me about being a tax auditor."

"It's along the lines of being a process server, bail bondsman, or oncologist."

Vlad laughed. "Is it that bad?"

"Sometimes it's fun. I get to learn about various businesses and professions and how they run financially. I also know all about which deductions are legal to take and under what circumstances."

"What if you catch someone taking illegal deductions?"

"Then he becomes a conservative politician."

Vlad guffawed. "I like the way you think."

They toasted with their red wine glasses.

"I've always been on the liberal side politically," Vlad said. "If we can't welcome everybody to the table, take care of each other and our environment, we're no better than the animals."

"Agreed." Jonathan sipped his wine. "What are your religious beliefs?"

Vlad considered the question. "I don't believe in all the mythology. So much of it seems to have been created by wealthy men to keep others under their thumb, and by the leaders of fat-cat organizations to raise money and not pay taxes."

"Until I audit them."

Vlad smiled. "I think if we look inward, we can tap into the spirit source. We can also find it when we help someone else, or when we fall in love."

"I like that." Jonathan winked at him. "Well, you know *my* beliefs."

"Do I ever." Vlad finished his dinner. "Speaking of which, I went a little too far in my acting today and my plastic fangs grazed a woman's neck, dripping real blood onto her white blouse."

"I can't believe I missed that!"

"I knew that would turn you on."

"It would have turned me on more if it was *my* neck."

Vlad chuckled. "You had yours at the cove the night we met."

"And just my luck, I fainted."

"That's because I'm such a good actor."

"Or a real descendant of Prince Vlad III, aka Dracula."

Vlad winked at him. "Maybe both."

"Now you're playing my song." Jonathan finished his dinner. "Do you have another acting job lined up for next week?"

"Never ask an actor that. We have a sore spot when it comes to unemployment."

"How come?"

"Probably because we're unemployed so much."

"Do you have any auditions coming up?"

Vlad sighed. "There are always auditions coming up. It's the good ones that are hard to get. And the jobs are even harder."

"I wonder if the same would hold true for a descendant of Dracula?"

Vlad shrugged. "I'll run it by my agent and let you know."

"Good." Jonathan then asked, "What's your apartment like in New York?"

"Small. But it's in a good neighborhood. Lots of butcher shops. How about your place in Trenton?"

"It's a condo on a lake with woods behind it."

"You must love that."

They shared a smile.

After finishing their desserts—sweet blood pudding for Vlad and blueberry cheesecake for Jonathan—they drove back to Cozzi Cove.

After Vlad parked his car, he noticed a parking sign had come down. So he lifted the poll and replaced it in the ground.

"Not many people could do that," Jonathan said.

Vlad smirked. "I know. I have supernatural strength because I'm a vampire."

"Does your father have your powers?"

"The only thing he lifts is the television remote control."

"Maybe it skipped a generation."

Walking along the dark cove, they gazed out at the twinkling stars protecting the charcoal lighthouse and onyx bay. When Vlad took Jonathan's small hand, it almost disappeared in his.

Not wanting to break the moment, but needing to know, Jonathan asked, "Have you thought any more about the whole gay-straight thing?"

Vlad nodded. "All last night and on my breaks during the day. I finally had a good talk with myself and decided to forget about all the labels—gay, straight, bi, vampire. Do what moves me. Be with who I like. And enjoy my time at Cozzi Cove."

"I like that decision."

"Me too."

They heard a howling sound, and then another, growing closer. They looked at each other as a third howl sounded. They continued walking on the cove toward the more private area in front of Bungalow Seven. Suddenly, what looked like a wolf stood in their path. It howled at the moon, and Jonathan gasped in fear. Vlad stared at the animal. It stared back, and then the animal ran away. When it was gone, Jonathan took in a few deep breaths.

"What *was* that thing?"

"A coywolf—half coyote and half wolf."

"How do you know?"

"I played a coywolf with bad breath in a TV commercial. I read they're pretty prevalent in New Jersey."

"I've never seen one before."

"Well, you saw one tonight."

Jonathan froze in place. "Vlad, do you realize what just happened?"

"We saw a coywolf."

"You used your ancestral powers. First, your superhuman strength to lift the parking poll, and again just now, to command the coywolf not to attack us."

Vlad walked in the other direction. "Whatever you say."

Jonathan followed. "I saw it, Vlad." When they arrived at Bungalow Three, Jonathan opened the door and Redfield and Barnabas flew into Vlad's arms. "See?"

Vlad petted the dogs. "I think you're exaggerating because you *want* me to have those powers."

"Whether I want it or not, you have them."

Vlad led the dogs into the kitchen and out the back door. He met up with Jonathan at the kitchen island.

"Would you like some tea?" Jonathan asked. "I have blood orange herbal."

"Very funny. Let's sit on the front porch."

They walked back through the living room to the porch and sat on the glider. Gazing at the mosaic of rocks, sand, and sky, Jonathan said, "It's going to be hard leaving this place in two days."

"On that we agree."

Jonathan turned to Vlad. "The hardest thing will be leaving you."

"We'll visit each other. Our dogs will have it no other way."

"You really want to see me after this week is over?"

"Is that so hard for you to believe?"

"It's been the norm in the past."

Vlad rested his hand on Jonathan's sunken cheek. "The past is the past. Right now, we're the present."

"Are we also the future?"

Vlad sighed. "I don't know. A few days ago I thought I was a straight mortal, remember?" Vlad giggled.

"What are you thinking?" Jonathan asked.

"To my surprise, how much I want to kiss you."

"Don't let me stop you."

Vlad slowly and softly took Jonathan into his arms for a warm, wet kiss.

Jonathan returned the kiss greedily.

To Jonathan's surprise, Vlad got up, took his hand, and led him into the front bedroom. Then Vlad lowered Jonathan onto the bed and lay on top of him. Vlad kissed, nibbled, licked, and sucked all over Jonathan's face and neck. Vlad awakened parts of his body he'd forgotten existed. Jonathan ran his hands through Vlad's long hair and down his lean back to finally squeeze Vlad's small, round bottom.

Vlad stopped kissing Jonathan and said, "I want to make love to you, but I don't know what to do."

Ecstatic, Jonathan replied, "It's been a very long time for me, but I remember taking off our clothes first."

Vlad yanked off his clothes, throwing them on the floor. Jonathan did the same.

"Now what?" Vlad asked, looking as if he would burst if they didn't make love.

Jonathan lowered Vlad onto his back and kissed his smooth forehead, stoic nose, and juicy lips. Then he ran his tongue along the side of Vlad's neck, around his erect nipples, inside the crease of each tiny abdominal muscle, and into his navel. He kissed and licked the dark mound of hair leading to Vlad's long, thin, curved, and throbbing dick. After licking his nuts, Jonathan deep-throated Vlad's dick. When Vlad cried out in elation, Jonathan sucked slowly and softly, and then as hard as he could. Vlad rested his hands on the back of Jonathan's head as he moaned and groaned in delight. When Jonathan tasted pre-cum, he sat up, pulled a lubed condom out of the night table drawer, and handed it to Vlad.

Vlad put it on quickly. "I know this part. It's what happens next I'm not too sure about."

Jonathan lay on his side, motioning for Vlad to spoon him, which he did quickly. Jonathan then reached out for Vlad's tool and slowly pressed it inside him. At first, the fit was quite tight, but after Jonathan cautiously leaned back into Vlad, he was able to relax and accept each of Vlad's gentle thrusts.

Vlad kissed him again and again as they found their rhythm. Then Vlad reached around for Jonathan's dick. As each of them was about to explode, Vlad leaned in and softly bit Jonathan on the neck, causing Jonathan to scream out in orgasm. Vlad followed quickly.

Vlad gasped in ecstasy and lay back on the bed. Jonathan, still curled into him, spooning, also lay panting for air. When Vlad found his voice, he said, "I've never experienced anything like that before. It was absolutely incredible."

"*You're* absolutely incredible, 'Count Dracula.'" Jonathan kissed Vlad.

"You're not so bad yourself, 'Jonathan Harker.'" They laughed as Vlad rolled on top of Jonathan, and they kissed and cuddled.

* * *

Just at that moment, Jesus, John, and Billy Dean passed by Bungalow Three, headed for John's car. Soon, they were at Carla's Seafood Restaurant, and as they entered, Billy Dean smiled at the nautical décor and netting overhead. A young woman introduced herself as Dotty and sat them at a table near a window.

After she went back to her welcome station, Billy Dean said to Jesus and John, "We don't have anything like this back home in Mobile."

"Cozzi is a special place," Jesus said.

In his dress shirt and slacks, blazer, and shined shoes, Billy Dean looked like he was out on a date. When the waitress arrived, Billy Dean ordered seafood chowder, lobster salad, and the fisherman's platter. Jesus and John each asked for minestrone, arugula and pear salad, and vegetable lasagna. Between the soup and salad courses, Billy Dean heard Jesus calling his name.

"Did I zone out?"

Jesus and John nodded.

"Sorry."

Jesus patted Billy Dean's hand. "Don't apologize."

"We're happy you could join us," John added.

Billy Dean started on his salad. "Y'all have been really nice to feed a big guy like me all week."

"How did your rehearsal go?" John asked.

"I'm doing fine with the singing, but the dancing has me a bit stumped," Billy Dean replied.

"John can help you with that," Jesus said.

John smiled. "I took some dance classes in college."

"That's terrific." Billy Dean rubbed his forehead. "And I have so many lines to learn."

"Jesus can assist you there." John rested a hand on Jesus's shoulder. "He had to memorize pages and pages of information for his nursing degree."

"Y'all are the best." Billy kissed them each on a cheek, not caring if anyone in the restaurant was watching.

When they had finished their dinners, they ordered desserts—chocolate cheesecake for Billy Dean and pineapple sorbet for Jesus and John.

Jesus cleared his throat. "Billy Dean, John and I have been talking about you."

Billy Dean blushed. "Have I been hanging around y'all too much?"

John smiled. "Quite the opposite."

"Did I miss an appointment with y'all?" Billy Dean asked.

Jesus slid forward in his chair. "We really like being with you, Billy Dean."

Billy Dean breathed a sigh of relief. "I really like being with y'all too!"

John rested his elbows on the table. "We more than like you, Billy Dean. I know that we've only known you a little less than a week, but we've grown quite attached to you."

"As a matter of fact, we both agreed that we're starting to fall in love with you," Jesus said.

Billy Dean did a double take. "I'm honored, and I would be lying if I didn't admit that I feel love for y'all. But you two are a couple."

Jesus nodded. "That's what we want to talk to you about."

"Y'all better not be breaking up," Billy Dean said.

"No," Jesus said. "John and I have been discussing the possibility of adding a third person to our family, should the right person come along."

"We've read a number of books on how people live in threesomes rather than couples," John added.

Billy Dean's head started to whirl. He wished he could talk to his grampa. "I don't know whether to check my backside or scratch my watch. What are y'all saying?"

Jesus took his hand. "Billy Dean, we think we found the right person. You."

John took Billy Dean's other hand. "The three of us fit. Jesus and I feel it. Don't you?"

Billy Dean nodded.

"When you're with us, we feel happy, excited, and safe. When you're not there, we're lonely, bored, and agitated, as if a part of us is missing," Jesus said.

"I feel the same way about y'all," Billy Dean said.

John squeezed his hand. "Then are you willing to take us up on our offer?"

"What offer?" Billy Dean asked.

"The three of us...living together...as a family," Jesus replied.

"You mean y'all would adopt me?"

"Billy Dean, we are asking you to live with us," Jesus said.

"As roommates?"

"No, as lovers, with equal rights," John said.

"You mean we'd live like a couple in love, only there'd be *three* of us?"

Jesus nodded. "We have plenty of room in our house. And it's close enough for you to commute to college."

"But people in love who live together are a couple." Billy Dean ran a hand through his hair. "Three people is a triangle."

"Not if they work at being a family, spend lots of time together, and make sure each person's needs are met," John answered.

"The books we've read mention having a date night each week, open communication, and regular family meetings to ensure everyone is heard, valued, and fulfilled," Jesus said.

John added, "It will be up to each of us to make sure we're all an equal part of the relationship."

"We never had any meetings in my house in Mobile. I was brought up to believe that a couple is a couple," Billy Dean said.

"We were brought up the same way." Jesus smiled. "And that the couple could only be a man and a woman. Our parents and our society were wrong about that. Maybe they're also wrong about committed lovers being only in groups of two."

"But you two have gotten a big head start as a couple," Billy Dean said. "How can I just join in?"

"We'll help you make up for lost time," John answered. "Both Jesus and I want you as our mate."

"Will you do us the honor of joining us, Billy Dean?" John asked.

It was as if a tornado had started at Billy Dean's heels and gone up to the tip of his head. Shaking all over, he got to his feet. "I have to go."

Jesus and John also stood. "What's wrong?"

"I'm sorry. Thank you for dinner." Billy Dean ran out of the restaurant before they could stop him. He took off down the block, turned a corner, and then raced down another block. It was as if the world had been turned upside down and was about to swallow him inside it. He ran until he spotted a familiar face through a glass window. Billy Dean whipped open the door of Tommy Malone's bar, rushed inside, and plopped down on a bar stool opposite Michael Rodgers. "I am lower than a raccoon in a garbage can."

"Come again?" Michael sat on a stool behind the bar.

Realizing Northerners didn't always understand his grampa's expressions, Billy Dean said, "I just ran out of Carla's Seafood Restaurant during a really nice meal with two terrific guys who have been treating me like royalty this week."

"Why?"

Billy Dean told Michael the entire story. When Billy Dean was finished, Michael rubbed his forehead.

"What are your concerns about Jesus and John's proposal?" Michael asked.

"What if I move in and they get tired of me? What if we have an argument? What if I get jealous? What if they get jealous? What if they get tired of me falling asleep more often than a bear in winter? What if they find out I can't find my behind with both hands in my pockets? How will I tell my family back in Mobile? How will I react if people make fun of me? When will I have any time to myself? When will I have any fun if I'm busy doing chores around the house?"

Michael seemed to weigh all the possibilities. "Couldn't all those things happen with a couple?"

Billy Dean's shoulders dropped. "I guess they could. But Jesus and John are eleven years older than me."

"Cal is eleven years older than me."

"Didn't it cause problems?"

"Mostly for Cal, not for me."

"How did he deal with it?"

"By realizing age doesn't define us. It's just a part of who we are. If you love someone, their age is simply part of the whole package." Michael leaned his elbows on the bar. "How do you feel about Jesus and John?"

"I think I'm falling in love with them."

"Both of them? Equally?"

Billy Dean nodded.

"Are you sure?"

Billy Dean nodded.

"Are they falling in love with *you*?"

"That's what they said at the restaurant." Billy Dean paused for a moment. "Even right now, I miss them like crazy, and I'll bet they're missing me. But they're *two* people!"

"Billy Dean, like you, I came from a home where the Bible was the law, and a man who loved another man was a sinner. It got me so crazy that I tried to gay bash Cal the day we met. But thanks to Cal's patience, I've completely reshaped everything I ever thought was true."

"But being in a relationship is a huge step, even for two people."

"Tell me about it. I've spent many nights wondering if I did the right thing by marrying Cal. And we've certainly had our share of disagreements. I've felt tempted to try other men. And I'm sure Cal has too. But in the end, I always realize I love Cal. And I don't want to be with anyone else." Michael wiped the bar with a rag. "I don't know what I would do if I were in your shoes, Billy Dean. But I've learned one thing—love is love. It's rare and precious. If it's real, you'll know when you have it. And if you do, you won't want to let it go."

It had gotten late, so Michael closed up the bar. He drove Billy Dean back to Cozzi Cove, where Billy Dean got on his bicycle and headed for his dorm with a hung head.

* * *

Cal jumped out of bed when Michael entered the front bedroom in the main bungalow.

Meeting him at the doorway, Cal stood in his boxers and asked, "Any word from Malcolm?"

Michael averted his gaze. "He stopped by Tommy's earlier."

"What did he say?"

Michael started undressing at the bureau. "He offered me a job."

"He did?"

Michael nodded.

Thrilled for his husband, Cal picked Michael up in his arms and spun him around in a circle. "That's terrific!"

When Michael landed on his feet, he said, "It's a photojournalist position to cover people in the entertainment industry."

Cal whistled. "Fancy. Does it mean going into New York City a lot?"

"Not exactly." Having stripped down to his boxers, Michael climbed into bed.

A cactus grew in Cal's stomach. "What aren't you telling me?"

Michael finally looked at Cal. "The job is in LA."

"LA? Los Angeles?"

"Well, it's not Louisiana, Cal."

Cal tried to stay calm. "What did you tell him?"

"I said I'd think about it and let him know tomorrow morning."

"And?"

"I'm thinking about it."

"You're willing to leave your husband and new baby for a job?"

"I didn't say that."

"Then what are you saying, Michael?"

"I'm saying I want to be with you and Cal Jr. But I also can't deny this job is a once-in-a-lifetime, outrageously amazing opportunity."

Cal climbed back into bed. "I was thinking the same thing."

"You were?"

Cal looked into Michael's dark, trusting eyes. "Don't you find it a bit coincidental that Malcolm came here grumbling about how I rejected him as a teenager, and now he offers you, with no experience, this dream job interviewing celebrities in LA?"

Michael said behind gritted teeth, "You're just like your sister, Cal. Everything always has to be about you."

"All right. Then maybe it's about *you*. Did you ever think that your future editor and mentor may have the hots for you?"

Michael clenched his fists to his forehead. "Why is it so hard for you to believe that I have talent?"

"I'm the one who brought you out of the alley and into my home, remember? The guy who gave you a job so you could go to college."

"*And* the guy who keeps throwing that in my face."

Cal put his hand on Michael's shoulder. "And I'm also the guy who loves you, married you, and is fathering a baby with you at Cozzi Cove, our home."

"*Your* home."

"It's your home too. Unless you go to LA with Malcolm."

Michael pressed his knees against his chest. "I don't want to leave you and the baby, but I keep wondering if there's some way we can work this out."

"You're the one who said long distance relationships don't work, Michael."

"But maybe we can figure out a way to make it work."

"Is that really what you want?"

"I don't know."

"Well figure it out fast, Michael. Carla is about to give us a child any day now. It would be nice if our son could have two parents, and if I could have a husband who isn't at the other end of the country."

Michael lay on the bed and turned his back to Cal.

Shocked at Michael's selfishness, Cal got out of bed, slipped on jeans and a T-shirt, and headed out the front door. Cal walked along the cove, filled with anger at Malcolm for filling Michael's head with pipe dreams, furious with Michael for taking Malcolm's bait, and enraged at himself for not stepping in sooner and putting an end to it. Tired from walking, he sat on a large rock and looked out at the cobalt sky hovering over the gray water. The lighthouse beam in the distance cast a dove-white glow over the bay.

Lance appeared next to him on the rock. He looked very like Michael.

"I miss you so much, Lance."

"Not as much as you used to. It'll get easier every year."

"I wish I could hold you in my arms."

"You know that's no longer possible."

Cal sighed. "Michael is so young."

"Like I was."

"But I'm older now, and losing my patience."

"You manage Cozzi Cove with great patience because you love it. Doesn't your young husband deserve the same?"

"You always knew what to say to calm me down." Cal smiled at his deceased husband. "I'm going to be a father."

"You'll need plenty of patience for that."

"I always thought we would share that together."

"We will. In a different way."

"I love Michael so much. I don't want to lose him, especially now."

Lance rose from the rock. "You won't. Michael is a part of you and a part of Cozzi Cove. Just like your memories of me." And then he was gone.

Cal returned to the main bungalow, took off his jeans and T-shirt, and climbed back into bed. Though Michael was still facing the wall, Cal knew his husband was awake. After taking a deep breath, Cal turned on the pin light at his night table and opened his great-grandfather's diary to the next entry.

August 1, 1937.

I know I have not written in a while. Things have been quite hectic. We are making great strides on Cozzi Cove, and many people have expressed an interest in staying with us when it is finished. We have also been meeting with the mayor to discuss future projects in town. You would think I would feel elated. To be honest, I have been quite sad lately. My assistant got married last week. As his employer and best friend, I stood up for him at the wedding, which pained me to no end. Throughout the church service and party afterward, I kept imaging it was us exchanging our vows, dancing the first dance, and feeding each other cake while everyone cheered. Of course it is not possible for two men to marry, and I doubt that it ever will be. I myself was married. And my assistant's young wife is a nice enough girl. But I must admit I continue to feel pangs of jealousy, knowing he shares his bed with her. On his wedding night, I thought I would go mad, envisioning him making love to her. He told me he still wants to visit and stay over at my house as much as possible. But how much longer will that last with a wife at home and no doubt a baby on the way soon? They have moved into his mother's house. He tells me his wife and his mother have grown quite close, and they hardly notice when he isn't there. The only times I feel whole and comforted are when he and I hold each other. And we have been able to do that less and less lately. Now I understand that love is the most powerful force on earth. It feels ephemeral and wonderful, but it is also hurtful and destructive.

As Cal fell asleep, he understood how his great-grandfather must have felt.

* * *

Michael spent most of the night tossing and turning, thinking about Malcolm's job offer. He woke the next morning having made his decision.

Since Cal was out shopping for supplies, Michael hadn't seen him that morning. So he put on a peach polo shirt and black shorts and headed out to Bungalow Two. Michael knocked, and Malcolm opened the door wearing white briefs that barely contained his huge package.

"When I said morning, I didn't mean sunrise."

"Is it too early?" Michael asked.

Malcolm yawned. "Come into the bedroom with me while I get dressed."

Michael followed Malcolm into the front bedroom, unable to stop staring at his sprawling back and bulbous buttocks.

When they got to the bedroom, Malcolm seemed to notice Michael staring at him. He smiled and wrapped his beefy arms around Michael.

"What are you doing?"

"Congratulating you on your job offer." Malcolm pressed Michael into his mountainous pecs.

Returning the hug, Michael smoothed his hands along Malcolm's rippling back muscles.

Malcolm took hold of Michael's hand and placed it inside Malcolm's briefs. Michael gasped at the touch of his enormous shaft and mushroom head as Malcolm planted a wet kiss on Michael's lips.

While kissing the incredibly good-looking older man was stimulating, Michael thought about Cal and their coming baby, and pushed Malcolm away.

"You want to play hard to get?"

"I don't want to play at all."

Malcolm chuckled. "That's not what your mouth and your hands just told me."

"You're an amazingly good-looking man, and I'm attracted to you. But nothing is going to happen between us."

"And why is that?"

"Because I'm married for one."

"I'm married too. But that shouldn't stop us from getting to know each other and working together."

"I'm in love with Cal, and he's all I want," Michael said.

"More than a career in photojournalism?"

It was as if he'd been hit in the stomach. "Is that what this is all about? Your offer to mentor me? The job in LA? Is it just a way for you and me to hook up?"

Malcolm rested a hand on Michael's shoulder. "Michael, I wasn't lying when I said you are a talented young man. And I think you can have a successful career in journalism. But there are lots of other talented young men out there. Every one of them is looking for the break I'm offering you." Malcolm walked over to the desk and pressed a button on his laptop. "I found an apartment for you in LA. It's within driving distance of mine."

Michael glanced at the pictures of the luxury apartment on the screen. "I could never afford that."

"I'll take care of that for you." Malcolm took Michael's hands and placed them on his huge pectoral muscles. "Don't lose out on this amazing deal, Michael. It's a once-in-a-lifetime offer."

Michael stepped back as if having burned his hands on hot charcoal. "The 'once-in-a-lifetime deal' is I become your young stud, and in return, you give me an apartment, a job, and some coaching?"

Malcolm sighed. "We don't need to define our relationship like that, Michael."

"I think we do, Malcolm. And since I'm the photographer, let me take a crack at it. The first shot is of you back at your apartment in New York or LA or wherever you live on the down-low. The next photo is of me here at Cozzi Cove with my family. No need to critique my work. I'm not making any changes, including hiding the gay content. And I'm keeping the caption picture. A photo of me, a gay black man."

Malcolm took a step back in obvious disbelief. "Do you know what you're passing up?"

"Yeah, I'm passing up you and your hypocrisy. Have a nice life, Malcolm." Michael left the bungalow.

Michael saw Cal returning from shopping and hurried to him. He threw himself into Cal's arms, sending Cal's bags onto the pavement. "I'm not going to LA. I want to be here with you and our baby."

Cal squeezed Michael so hard that Michael lost his breath. "You and the baby are my life. You mean everything to me."

"I'm yours forever."

They kissed again and again.

Michael looked at the rumpled bags on the ground. "I hope nothing's broken."

"I don't care."

They kissed again.

Suddenly, a woman's piercing scream came from Bungalow One.

Michael and Cal broke apart and looked at each other, eyes wide. "Carla!"

They had just turned to hasten toward the bungalow when a car spun into the Cozzi Cove lot, gravel spitting from its wheels. Sandra, Carla's midwife, jumped out and hurried along the pavement in front of the bungalows, carrying a large black bag.

"Carla called me five minute ago when her water broke," she said to them breathlessly.

"Do you have everything you need?" Cal asked.

Sandra pointed to her bag. "Birthing equipment, baby monitoring devices, and sterilizing apparatus all here. Get me some freshly laundered towels and sterilized water."

Michael and Cal let Sandra into Bungalow One, and the midwife dashed into the back bedroom. The two men then raced to the hall closet where Michael grabbed towels and Cal pulled out a basin and a jug of sterilized water.

As Michael and Cal entered Carla's bedroom, they placed the towels, and the basin and water on the desk, and Sandra opened her black bag.

"Is it time?" Cal asked.

Carla's eyes were bloodshot. Sweat poured down her face. She held on to the night table and screamed, "You think, Cal?"

Michael hurried around the other side of the bed and took Carla's hand. "Remember your meditating, auras, and chakras."

"Screw all that! Get this thing out of me!"

The midwife reminded Carla to do her breathing cycles as she led Cal and Michael out of the room. "I'll call you when the baby arrives."

In the doorway, Cal said, "It seems like that will be soon."

"Not soon enough!" Carla screeched from her bed.

The midwife shut the bedroom door.

Taylor, fresh off her plane, chose that moment to enter from the front of the house and met up with Cal and Michael in the living room. "I appreciate you both being here for my arrival, but some breakfast would be nice."

A guttural shriek came from the bedroom.

Taylor looked at Cal, and Cal nodded.

"I have terrible cramps," Taylor said, moaning, and she sat at the kitchen table and held her stomach.

Cal and Michael joined her at the table.

"Sandra said she'll tell us when the baby arrives," Cal said.

Carla screamed from the bedroom, "It's him or me!"

"Why does she have to be so dramatic?" Taylor rocked back and forth. "I feel like my stomach is going to explode."

Sandra called out from the bedroom, "He's making an entrance."

Michael, Cal, and Taylor rushed into the room and stood a few feet away from the bed.

Sandra said, "Breathe, Carla! Now push!"

Carla braced her back against the headboard and let out a guttural moan.

"Again," Sandra said.

With her face as red as a strawberry, Carla sucked in some air and groaned as she pushed.

"One more time, Carla," Sandra said.

The third time was the winner. Carla screamed, and Sandra lifted the baby from the bed sheets.

Michael and Cal held each other and wept. Taylor used one of the towels to wipe her own brow.

Sandra cut the umbilical cord, and everyone exhaled in relief at the sound of the baby's first wail. Sandra cleaned the baby, wrapped him in a blanket on the bed, and placed various monitoring devices on his chest, back, and head.

"Is the baby all right?" Cal asked Sandra.

Sandra checked the meters on her equipment. "He seems as strong as a horse."

"You're telling me!"

"Are you okay?" Michael asked Carla.

"I am now." Carla wiped the perspiration off her forehead with a towel and reached out for Taylor.

Taylor sat at the edge of the bed, took Carla's hand, and said, "I feel faint."

Sandra replied, "There are smelling salts in my bag."

Taylor reached into the bag and placed a packet under her nose.

Once Sandra seemed satisfied with the baby's health, she cleaned him again, and applied oil to his rosy skin. After placing him in another blanket, she handed him to Cal.

Cal cradled his son in his arms, and the baby stopped crying. As Cal gently held the newborn, he motioned for Michael to join him. Michael placed his arms around Cal's, and the new family embraced for the first time.

"He's so tiny," Michael said.

"He smiled at us." Cal kissed his baby's cheek. "Hello little Cal. I'm your papa."

"And I'm your daddy," Michael added, kissing his baby's other cheek.

Sandra said, "The baby should have some nourishment as soon as possible."

Carla groaned. "Oh, goody."

Cal brought the baby to Carla and placed him on her chest. As Carla breast fed him, Taylor said, "My nipples are sore."

Sunbeams filled the room, bathing it in gold and amber. Cal and Michael stood arm in arm, beaming with pride. The next generation was born at Cozzi Cove.

CHAPTER TEN

That same morning, since there had been so much commotion in Bungalow One, Billy Dean had started at Bungalow Two. He cleaned and restocked all the other bungalows, as usual leaving Bungalow Seven for last. Now, he stood in front of the door with his maid's cart and waited until John answered his knock. The dark circles under John's eyes matched his T-shirt and shorts.

Billy Dean said, "I hope I didn't wake you."

John shook his head. "We were up most of the night. Come on in."

As he entered, Billy Dean noticed Jesus just getting out of bed. "What's wrong?"

Jesus threw on his robe and joined them in the living room. "We were worried about you."

"And Jesus had a bad night," John added.

Billy Dean placed his head in his hands. "I'm sorry I ran out on y'all last night."

"Are you okay?" Jesus asked. "Please have a seat."

"Not really," Billy Dean said as he complied. "I'm really honored and proud that two such wonderful people love me and want to make a family with me. And I love the both of you, and I want to be with you too."

"But?" Jesus sat on the sofa.

"I was raised to believe that love is a sacred bond between two people culminating in marriage and children," Billy Dean replied.

John sat next to Jesus. "The people who picket the funerals that the Angels shield believe the same thing."

"I know you don't understand. I don't fully understand it myself." Billy Dean sighed. "The thought of walking away from you is tearing me up inside. But I don't want to come between you two."

"But you'd be *joining* us," Jesus said.

Tears filled Billy Dean's eyes. "No, I won't. I've thought about this all night and all morning. And that's my decision. I'm sorry."

"Are you sure?" Jesus asked.

Billy Dean nodded.

"Can the three of us still be friends?" John asked.

"I don't think that's a good idea," Billy Dean replied.

As Billy Dean rose, Jesus and John enveloped him in their arms. The three of them shared a long embrace.

Billy Dean broke the huddle; his heart was broken. "I'd better get my cart and clean this place."

Jesus took John's hand. "We'll be out at the cove."

Tears stained Billy Dean's eyes as he cleaned and restocked the bungalow. Then he walked across the cove and left his maid's cart in the supply shed. He mounted his bicycle and headed back to his dorm with Jesus and John looking after him sadly in front of Bungalow Seven.

* * *

That evening, sitting at the patio table of Bungalow Five, Andrew finished his last delicious forkful of Nijad's casserole of chicken, artichokes, tomatoes, prunes, lemon, olive oil, and sesame seeds over brown rice. The prior evening, Andrew had made them whole wheat pizza topped with broccoli, asparagus, jumbo shrimp, and three cheeses along with a Caesar salad.

Nijad took Andrew's hand. "I'm so glad I met you."

Andrew kissed Nijad's hand. "You read my mind. I was thinking the same thing."

After they shared a long kiss, Nijad looked up at the periwinkle sky.

"What are you thinking about?" Andrew asked.

"I was wondering why we haven't heard from Annabel this evening? I hope...she doesn't...feel as if she can't be...herself."

"Nijad, if this is going to work, we both need to be honest with each other. I don't want you to be afraid of hurting my feelings. And I would feel terrible if I hurt yours again. So let's *both* be honest. Annabel is a part of me, but I know that most people, though they have different facets to their personality, don't have alters. And now that my mother is no longer a part of my life, and the gay bashing is in my past, I understand Annabel is fulfilling some other need inside me. Perhaps it's a method of reaching out to others and feeling more comfortable with people like you. I believe I'll know the answers after more sessions with my psychiatrist. But please be honest with me. Are you freaked out about Annabel? Would you prefer not to see her again?"

Nijad sat back in his seat, deliberating Andrew's question. "I'm not accustomed to this."

"Of course you aren't."

"And it's taking some getting used to."

"Annabel appearing and disappearing?"

Nijad nodded. "And I enjoy our time together so much."

"But do you also enjoy your time with Annabel?"

Nijad smiled. "I think I do."

"Because, unlike me, Annabel is vivacious, sexy, and madcap?"

"No, because Annabel is a part of you. And I love you."

Andrew lost his breath. "I love you too."

They shared a sweet kiss. Then Nijad rose, scooped Andrew into his arms, and carried him inside to the front bedroom. After laying Andrew on the bed, Nijad took off their dress shirts and slacks. Then lying on top of Andrew, he took Andrew's face in his hands, and they kissed again and again. Nijad rubbed his groin into Andrew's until Andrew couldn't hold back any longer. He slipped off his underpants, and Nijad did the same. As their naked bodies pressed against each other, an invisible dam opened and the pain in Andrew's life slowly oozed out of his body.

Andrew kissed Nijad's prominent nose and the cleft in his chin. He squeezed Nijad's wide pectoral muscles. Nijad licked and flicked his tongue inside Andrew's ear and over his neck until Andrew gasped in excitement. Nijad worked his way down Andrew's lean stomach and took Andrew inside his mouth. He then licked and sucked at the long, thin shaft and head while rubbing his balls. Andrew, the tension ramping up in him, reached for the back of Nijad's head and pulled at his thick dark locks. Just as Andrew was about to cry out in ecstasy, Nijad hoisted himself over his lover and lowered his dick into Andrew's mouth. His jaw aching, Andrew worked to accommodate the massive tool, while Nijad reached into the night table drawer for a lubed condom. As he became more accustomed to Nijad's size, Andrew sucked and slurped contentedly and ran his tongue along Nijad's foreskin. Nijad, clearly not able to wait any longer, suited up, raised Andrew's legs, and then slowly and very gently entered him. Andrew screamed out in pain, but after a few moments, the pain turned into deep, deep pleasure, and Nijad penetrated him more fully. With each thrust, Nijad reached inside

Andrew's heart and touched every emotion within him. He seemed to understand Andrew's fears, disappointments, and agonies, and like a miracle man, exorcised them with his love.

Andrew squeezed Nijad's sculpted back, working his way down to Nijad's firm, full bottom and powerful thighs.

After they kissed and caressed for some time, Annabel said, "This is the best shag I've ever had!"

"Me too." Nijad kissed Annabel's neck and nibbled on her nipples. When Annabel cried out in pleasure, Nijad built up his intensity and rhythm.

Just as they were about to climax, Nijad said, "I want Andrew."

Andrew kissed him. "Nijad, I want you so much."

Gazing into Andrew's eyes, Nijad grasped his penis and rubbed forcefully.

Moments later, Nijad slipped off the condom, and they both shouted out as their orgasms erupted onto each other's chests.

Nijad dropped to the bed to lie on his back panting. Andrew rested his head on Nijad's heaving chest and said, "I'm so happy I found you."

Nijad kissed Andrew's forehead. "I'm so happy I found you too. The both of you."

They nestled together and fell asleep in each other's arms.

* * *

In the front bedroom of the bungalow next door, Jonathan and Vlad lay in bed. The last day of the convention had ended with Vlad, as Dracula, pretend-biting a young woman's neck using his plastic fangs. Then he raised his black cape above his face, and disappeared from the convention hall—courtesy of a flash pot, a black curtain, and a trap door. Afterward, Jonathan and Vlad had dinner at the diner in town—blood rare roast beef for Vlad and turkey pot pie for Jonathan—and then they went for a walk on the cove that led them back to Vlad's bungalow.

As they lay in bed naked together, Jonathan asked, "How are you doing with all this?"

Vlad put his arm around Jonathan. "You tell me."

Jonathan giggled. "I think you're doing just fine."

"I think you're doing just fine too."

After a deep, warm, wet kiss, Jonathan rested his hands on Vlad's chest. "But there's just one thing."

"What's that?" Vlad asked with concern showing on his chiseled face.

"Can you bite me harder on the neck?"

Vlad smiled. "I think we can work something out."

Vlad lay on top of Jonathan, and they kissed again. Jonathan broke away and moved the long black hair away from Vlad's face and said, "I'm falling in love with you."

"With me, or with Dracula?"

"Definitely with you."

"I'm falling in love with you too."

"Does it frighten you?"

"Not anymore. Regardless of what I was in the past, you're the one I want now."

They kissed again, and then Vlad slipped on a lubed condom, flipped Jonathan onto his stomach, penetrated him from behind, and they made passionate love. As Jonathan and Vlad built up their rhythm and intensity, Vlad reached for Jonathan's dick, kissed Jonathan's cheek, and then bit into his neck. They shouted out their orgasms and then fell onto their sides into each other's arms.

After more kissing and fondling, clearly concerned, Vlad examined Jonathan's neck. "Did I draw blood?"

Jonathan sat up and looked at his reflection in the bureau mirror. "No," he added with a shiver of delight, "but you left two red marks from your molars."

Vlad sat up next to Jonathan, and they shared a lengthy kiss.

"Oh my God!"

"What is it?"

In a state of shock, Jonathan pointed to the bureau mirror. "There's only my reflection. Yours isn't there!"

Vlad looked at the mirror. "That's because you're in front of the mirror and I'm not."

Jonathan rested against the bed's headboard. "I think there's more to it than that."

Vlad joined Jonathan. "I know you think I have vampire genes. But to me, it's mythology. I'm not suddenly going to sleep in a coffin all day and suck people's blood by night."

"You looked pretty convincing coming out of that coffin at the Horror Convention."

"It smelled like moth balls. I couldn't wait for my cue to exit."

"And you seemed right at home biting me just now when we were making love."

"You asked me to do that."

Renfield and Barnabas entered the bedroom and rested their heads on the bed next to Jonathan and Vlad. Vlad made eye contact with them, and the two dogs quickly lay under the bed together.

"See?" Jonathan said, "Vlad, I think you need to fully embrace your heritage."

Vlad kissed Jonathan's chin. "Will you still love me, even though I'm not a vampire?"

"Vlad, I'm honored and delighted and quite frankly in total shock that you like me. Even if you never ate another bite of bloody meat, lost your allergy to garlic, and became a sun worshiper, I'd still love you. Because I love *you*, Vlad Lesti." Jonathan added, "Descended from Prince Vlad III of the House of Draculesti. And I think you need to claim that for all the world to see."

"How?"

"Did you call your agent and tell him about this?"

Vlad nodded. "So far it hasn't helped my career any."

"I have a feeling that will change soon."

"Your sixth sense again?"

"Which I've fully embraced. As I've embraced you." Jonathan kissed Vlad's cheek.

"I don't know about the vampire thing. But there's one thing I do know. Whether I'm gay, bi, or gay curious, I love you for the funny, warm, supportive, and adorable man you are, Jonathan Harker." Vlad placed his fingers over his lips. "I mean, Jonathan Harper."

"I liked it better the first time, Count Dracula."

They laughed wickedly and lay back down on the bed, sharing a long embrace.

* * *

Out on the cove, the laughter Cal heard coming from Bungalow Four matched his giddy state as he carried the baby and Michael carried bottles of Carla's pumped milk to the main bungalow. Michael had had someone cover for him at the bar and he and Cal had spent most of the day in Bungalow One watching the baby cry, feed, or sleep. They both had thanked Carla profusely, despite Taylor's indifference to anything Carla might have contributed to the birth of "Taylor's nephew."

Upon entering their bungalow, Cal and Michael made their way to the rear bedroom and carefully placed the baby in his crib.

They both stood beaming down at this newest addition to their family, and then Cal turned to Michael and said joyously, "We have a baby!"

Michael threw his arms around his husband and they shared a long, jubilant kiss. "I'm glad I turned down Malcolm's job offer. We're a family now."

"I love you so much." Cal hugged Michael hard to his chest.

Just then, Michael's cell phone buzzed. He pulled away and checked the screen. "I have a job interview on Skype tomorrow morning."

"That's terrific! You'd better get some rest."

"You first. I'll take the second sleep shift."

After kissing his baby's pink cheek, Cal headed for the front bedroom to get some sleep, as Michael spent the first half of the night sitting by the baby's crib.

Later, fully rested for his shift, Cal kissed his baby's forehead and gazed at his beautiful child sleeping soundly. Then he sat in the rocking chair next to the crib. When Cal's eyelids started to droop, he opened his great-grandfather's diary and read the final entries under the floor lamp next to his chair.

December 25, 1937.

Things have been in such a whirlwind, but I had to do a diary entry on Christmas. Cozzi Cove and all the furnishings are built. It has surpassed all of my and my assistant's hopes. I am moving into the main bungalow this spring and opening the others for business this summer. I am so proud that my little boy will grow up on the beach as I did.

My assistant and I will start building in town this spring. If all goes well, he may be right, and they will rename the town after me. His wife is large with child and should be giving birth sometime this summer. He is thrilled to be a father, and he asked me for some tips on fatherhood, which I was happy to share with him. As I expected, we have found less and less time to share my bed. Doc Robinson says my assistant has asthma, which makes me worry about him. I admit that

I fall asleep many nights longing for his embrace, warm breath on my cheek, and welcoming smile.

June 3, 1938.

My last diary entry is exactly one year after starting it. I have not written since I have not yet recovered from that horrible day last month. My assistant asked me if I would like to go to the main beach with him. I declined, being too busy preparing things at Cozzi Cove. He swam out into the sea and never came back. Was it the asthma that winded him while swimming, causing him to panic for breath in the water and drown? Was it a freak accident? Did a shark get him? Or did he decide that this world was not a good place for men like him and me to live in? His body has never been found, and I will never know.

Cozzi Cove is opening this week for business, which makes me proud, and makes me think of my assistant. The stores that my assistant and I built in town are nearly completed, and merchants have contacted me to rent them. My little boy is walking and climbing all over our bungalow. He will be playing on the rocks at Cozzi Cove in no time.

My assistant's wife just gave birth to a beautiful baby boy who looks very much like his father. Seeing him brought a tear to my eye. I wish his father could see him too.

As I sit on a rock at Cozzi Cove and look out at the crystal clear water leading to the pale blue sky and the stoic lighthouse in the distance, I wonder if there will be a day when men like my assistant and me can be together without fear of ridicule, loss of status, danger, and imprisonment. However, I do know one thing. I never have and never will again love anyone like I loved my friend. I carry him in my mind and heart, and I will think of him always with every breath that I take. Cozzi Cove is as much his creation and lifeblood as mine. Since he is no longer with us in Cozzi, New Jersey, I will end by dedicating my diary and the rest of my life to Michael Rodgers.

* * *

The next morning, Cal cleaned, fed, kissed, and rocked the baby in the back bedroom while Michael showered, dressed, ate, and had his Skype job interview.

Meeting in the baby's room, Cal asked Michael, "How did your interview go?"

Michael shrugged. "I answered their questions and e-mailed them my work."

The baby wailed. Michael took over baby duties, as Cal washed and dressed in a canary T-shirt and denim shorts, and then ate breakfast.

He entered the back bedroom and handed Michael the diary. "You may want to read this."

"Why?" Michael asked as the baby spat up on his mauve polo shirt.

"Trust me. The ending's a shocker."

Michael wiped the baby's mouth and placed him in his crib. Picking up the diary, he sat on the rocking chair and opened it.

Hearing the front door open, Cal hurried into the living room to stand behind his desk. He locked eyes with Malcolm Wolf who stood just inside the doorway in a tan leisure suit with gold jewelry dripping off him and his designer luggage at his feet.

Without a word, Malcolm handed Cal the bungalow key. Cal couldn't have been happier to have the magazine editor leave.

Malcolm looked around Cal's living room. "This place certainly has changed."

Still fuming from Michael's recap of Malcolm's pass from the day before, Cal replied, "But it's still a place where honesty and commitment mean something." He glared at Malcolm. "As you found out yesterday in your bungalow."

Malcolm smiled. "As the saying goes, 'there are plenty of other young photojournalists in the unemployment pool.'"

"Hopefully there aren't too many other editors like you ready to exploit them."

"You haven't changed much, Cal. You're still uptight and judgmental."

"And I'm still not interested in *you*. Neither is my husband."

Malcolm picked up his bag. "You have a beautiful place and a good husband."

"I plan to keep it that way."

Cal walked Malcolm to the door and happily watched him leave Cozzi Cove, pretty certain he would never return.

While standing in the doorway of the main bungalow, Cal couldn't help overhearing his new employee and two of his guests talking outside.

Looking like a sad beagle, Billy Dean stood next to the shed and opposite Jesus Santiago and John DeDeo. He said, "Grampa would think me ruder than a cussing preacher if I didn't say good-bye to y'all."

Smiling morosely, Jesus put down his bag and rested a hand on Billy Dean's shoulder. "It's been wonderful getting to know you. I wish you all the best life has to offer."

Clearly forlorn, John also put down his bag and placed his hand on Billy Dean's other shoulder. "You're a wonderful young man. Godspeed."

Jesus and John picked up their bags and headed toward their car.

"Wait!" Billy Dean ran to them. "I don't want to lose you."

Jesus rested his palm on Billy Dean's cheek. "Have you changed your mind about being our friend?"

"No, I've changed my mind about being your lover." Billy Dean turned to John. "And I want to be your lover too."

"Are you serious?" Jesus asked.

"As serious as a mouse in a cheese factory," Billy Dean replied.

Jesus and John brought Billy Dean in for a long three-way kiss. "Come to our house for dinner after your rehearsal tonight, and we'll talk about it."

"I don't want to come for dinner. I want to move in," Billy Dean said. "I don't care how I was raised or what other people will think. I don't care if you'll get tired of me, or if I'll never have a minute to myself, or if we argue all the time. I don't care if I have to do chores, or even if I get jealous or if you find out I'm a loser. I just want to be with y'all!"

Jesus and John kissed each other, and then they each kissed Billy Dean. "We want that too."

"I'm glad. I'll bike over tonight with my things." Billy Dean smiled.

"We'll be there." Jesus and John hugged him.

As Jesus and John got into John's car with their bags, Jesus said, "We'll be cozier than three turtles on a lily pad."

"I'm happier than a tick on an overweight dog," John added.

The three of them laughed, and then Jesus and John drove off.

Cal also spotted Nijad Hadad and Andrew Urban, both wearing polo shirts and shorts, leaving Bungalow Five and Six respectively with their bags in hand and walking toward the main bungalow.

Cal hurried behind his desk and smiled at Nijad and Andrew as they entered the living room. "I hope you enjoyed your stay at Cozzi Cove."

Andrew handed Cal the two keys. "More than we ever thought possible."

Looking from one to the other, he said, "It seems like you both made a new friend."

Nijad's dark eyes glistened. "Yes, we made friends."

"See you for lunch at my place," Andrew said to Nijad.

"I'm looking forward to it," Nijad replied following up with a kiss.

"Will it be all right if Annabel makes an appearance?"

"That would be just fine."

They shared a smile, and with a nod to Cal, headed out of the bungalow with bags in hand, passing the next departing guests.

Vlad Lesti wore a black shirt, pants, and cape, and sported a large ruby ring on his finger. A cane with a small skull at the top and sunglasses completed his ensemble. He turned to Jonathan Harper next to him and said, "I got a call on my cell from my agent. He got me an audition for tomorrow to play a modern-day vampire in an indie movie."

"That's terrific!" Jonathan replied.

"Since I'm a method actor, I'll be working on the role tonight. You want to stay over in the city and help me?"

Jonathan giggled joyously. "You better believe it!"

Renfield and Barnabas followed their masters into the living room as the two men walked to the desk and turned in their keys.

Cal took the keys and smiled. "It looks like Cozzi Cove made another match."

"Actually, two matches." Vlad put his arm around Jonathan, and Barnabas rested a paw on Renfield's face.

Laughing, Cal said, "I hope you'll come again, Mr. Lesti and Mr. Harper."

Vlad spun his cape and replied, "That's 'Count Dracula' and 'Jonathan Harker.'" He kissed Jonathan on the neck, leaving a red mark. With a wave at Cal, they left the office followed by their pets.

With all the guests checked out, Cal went to join Michael and the baby in the back bedroom. Meanwhile, Carla and Taylor had arrived through the back of the bungalow and now sat on the two rocking chairs in the bedroom. The baby cried intermittently as Cal and Michael took turns holding him.

"How are you feeling?" Cal asked Carla.

"A lot better since junior made his entrance." Carla reached over and kissed Taylor's cheek. "And since my wife turned down the job in Paris."

"What changed your mind, sis?"

Taylor gazed at the baby. "My nephew. After all I've done to bring him into the world, I couldn't face the thought of leaving him."

Carla groaned. "Would it hurt my karma if I murdered Taylor the day after I gave birth?"

Michael laughed and then he asked Taylor, "Are you going to keep consulting?"

"I got another job offer as the CFO for a financial management firm." Taylor smiled at Carla. "And I accepted."

"It's in New York City." Carla beamed like a lighthouse. "A lot closer to home."

Michael replied, "Can we carpool, sister-in-law?"

Taylor looked at Michael as if he had suggested they open a newsstand together. "Come again?"

"I interviewed on Skype this morning, and I just accepted a job as a junior photojournalist for a gay magazine in the city," Michael said.

"I'm so proud of you!" Cal said as he kissed Michael all over his face.

Taylor sighed. "I suppose you'll want me to take you to lunch some days."

Michael winked at her. "When my schedule allows." He took the baby from Cal.

Rising slowly, Carla looked at her nephew and then at Michael and Cal. "He looks like both of you."

Taylor joined her wife. "I think he looks like me."

"Like Cozzi Cove, he's a part of *all* of us." Cal smiled at Michael. "And our great-grandfather's diary explains why."

After Cal and Michael filled them in, Carla asked Cal, "So your great-grandfather and Michael's great-grandfather built Cozzi Cove in 1937?"

Cal nodded and put his arm around Michael. "Cozzi Cove is a part of Michael's birthright too."

Taylor blew a kiss at Michael. "We'll keep the deed in Cal's name." She rubbed her finger against the baby's cheek. "Have you thought about having a baptism?"

"Asked the woman who hasn't set foot in a church in years," Cal said.

Taylor adjusted the collar of her cerulean business suit. "Just because I don't go to church doesn't mean I'm not religious. I've made a ton of money investing for churches. Synagogues and mosques too. We ought to look into turning Cozzi Cove into a church. The tax-exempt status is a godsend."

"I'm not bringing my son to an organization that lobbies against my marriage and family," Cal replied.

"There are some open and affirming churches," Michael said.

"I wouldn't waste my time with them," Taylor said. "They generally don't have the big bucks and political connections that the antigay churches have."

Carla grasped at the dangling crystal at her neck that matched her violet kimono with a picture of the planets on the front. "I have an idea!"

Later that afternoon, Cal, Michael, Taylor, and Carla welcomed local bar owner Tommy Malone and his girlfriend Blue Magnum to Cozzi Cove. The couple was handsome in a black suit and a chartreuse wraparound satin dress respectively. Arriving at the same time were Cal and Taylor's half-brother George Valis and his husband Aaron Weiss, both in navy blue suits. Clad in white suits, Cal and Michael held their baby, dressed in a white ruffled tunic, and led the way to the white sand at Cozzi Cove. With the sun radiating its glow over the crystal blue sky and water beneath it, the group formed a semicircle around Cal, Michael, and their baby.

As the foamy bay water inched closer to their feet, Carla bent down, scooped a handful, and gently poured it over the baby's forehead. "Here at Cozzi Cove—"

"Our home," Michael said with a smile toward Cal.

"May the bay water cleanse you." Carla raised her crystal and the sun shined rainbow beams over the infant. "May the sun keep you warm. The rocks protect you. The sand ground you. And may the lighthouse beam your path to health and happiness."

"And success," Taylor added.

"We the residents of Cozzi Cove baptize you Calvin Michael Rodgers Cozzi," Cal said.

"Blessed be," Michael replied.

Everyone shouted "Amen!"

The couples each kissed. Cal and Michael kissed their baby. And the owners of Cozzi Cove looked out over the sparkling bay.

ABOUT THE AUTHOR

Joe Cosentino was voted Favorite LGBT Mystery, Contemporary, and Humorous Novelist of 2015 by the readers of Divine Magazine, and Second Place Favorite LGBT Romance Novelist. The first book in the Cozzi Cove book series, *Cozzi Cove: Bouncing Back*, was voted Favorite Book of the Month by The TBR Pile and received an Honorable Mention Rainbow Award. One of many for Joe. Other books in the Cozzi Cove series published by NineStar Press are *Cozzi Cove: Moving Forward* and *Cozzi Cove: Stepping Out*.

Joe also authored the Nicky and Noah mystery novels (Lethe Press): *Drama Queen, Drama Muscle, Drama Cruise*, and *Drama Luau*; the Jana Lane mystery novels (The Wild Rose Press): *Paper Doll, Porcelain Doll, Satin Doll China Doll*, and *Rag Doll*; and the romance novellas (Dreamspinner Press): *In My Heart/An Infatuation & A Shooting Star, A Home for the Holidays*, and *The Naked Prince and Other Tales from Fairyland*.

As an actor, Joe has appeared in principal roles in film, television, and theatre, opposite stars such as Bruce Willis, Rosie O'Donnell, Nathan Lane, Jason Robards, and Holland Taylor. He received his Master of Fine Arts degree and Master's degree, and is currently a happily married college professor/department head residing in New York State.

Website: http://www.JoeCosentino.weebly.com
Facebook: http://www.facebook.com/JoeCosentinoauthor
Twitter: @JoeCosen
Goodreads blog:
https://www.goodreads.com/author/show/4071647.Joe_Cosentino

ALSO BY JOE COSENTINO

Cozzi Cove series:

Cozzi Cove: Bouncing Back
Cozzi Cove: Moving Forward
Cozzi Cove: Stepping Out

NINESTAR PRESS, LLC

www.ninestarpress.com

www.ingramcontent.com/pod-product-compliance
Lightning Source LLC
Chambersburg PA
CBHW050945120626
46552CB00001B/396